Alexis

and the

perfect

recipe

This book is a work of fiction. Any references to historical events, real people, or real places are used fictitiously. Other names, characters, places, and events are products of the author's imagination, and any resemblance to actual events or places or persons, living or dead, is entirely coincidental.

SIMON SPOTLIGHT

An imprint of Simon & Schuster Children's Publishing Division

1230 Avenue of the Americas, New York, New York 10020

Copyright © 2011 by Simon & Schuster, Inc.

First Simon Spotlight hardcover edition 2013

All rights reserved, including the right of reproduction in whole or in part in any form.

SIMON SPOTLIGHT and colophon are registered trademarks of Simon & Schuster, Inc.

Text by Elizabeth Doyle Carey

Chapter header illustrations and design by Laura Roode

For information about special discounts for bulk purchases, please contact Simon & Schuster Special Sales at 1-866-506-1949 or business@simonandschuster.com.

Manufactured in the United States of America 0413 FFG

First Edition

2 4 6 8 10 9 7 5 3 1

ISBN 978-1-4424-7493-2 (hc)

ISBN 978-1-4424-2901-7 (pbk)

ISBN 978-1-4424-2902-4 (eBook)

Library of Congress Control Number 2011929623

Alexis

and the

perfect

recipe

by coco simon

Simon Spotlight

New York   London   Toronto   Sydney   New Delhi

CHAPTER 1

My Sister Takes the Cake

My name is Alexis Becker, and I'm the business mind (ha-ha) of the Cupcake Club. The club is a for-profit group that my best friends—Mia, Katie, and Emma—and I started, and we make money baking delicious cupcakes!

I love figuring out how to run a business and putting together the different building blocks—math, organization, planning—that's why the girls can *count* on me for this kind of stuff. Plus, as you can tell, I love math-related puns! My friends are more creative with the cupcakes, so they come up with the designs and other artistic stuff. My one specialty, though, is fondant. I am very good at making little flowers and designs out of that firm frosting. Otherwise, I'm mostly crunching numbers and wondering how to make money. Mmm . . . money!

If the Cupcake Club was an equation, it would look like this:

$$(4 \text{ girls} + \text{supplies}) \times \text{clients} = \$\$\$\$$$

Or really, more like this:

$$(\text{Profit} - \text{supplies}) / 4 = \$$$

We actually have lots of fun doing it. Most of our clients are really nice people, which is much more than I can say for our latest client: my sister, Dylan. I can practically still hear her fuming.

"It is *my* party, *I* am the one turning sixteen, and I have budgeted *everything* down to the last party favor. I know *exactly* what I'm doing!" She was talking to our mom behind closed doors, but I heard every word since I was right outside her bedroom!

Dylan never gets out-of-control mad; she's always in total control. Except that ever since she'd started planning her sweet sixteen party (which was now four and a half weeks away), she'd been cranky *a lot*. But she never raises her voice when she gets mad. She lowers it to a whisper, and you can hear the chill in it as if actual icicles were hanging from the words. I had to put my ear to her bedroom door to hear everything that was being said. Knowledge is power; that's one of my mottoes, and I need all the information I can get. About everything.

My mother was sounding kind of amused by the fight, which was about two things: the guest list for the party and the cake. I had an interest in the outcome of both, since I wanted to be able to invite my best friends, and *we* wanted to bake the dessert for the party. (It wasn't about the money as we wouldn't charge a lot; it's just that it would be great exposure for our business!)

I could picture Mom trying not to smile and to take Dylan seriously. "Darling, I know how careful you are, and I am impressed, as always, by your work," she said. "I admire your attention to detail on these spreadsheets. However, not everything will be according to *your* plan, as your father and I also have a say in what works best for this family. Now let's take a look at this guest list again."

I grinned. Mom was on *my* side.

There were some muffled comments and I strained to hear them. Maybe I'd hear better if I put

3

a glass against the wall like I'd seen people do on TV. Or maybe I should lie down and listen through the crack under the door. I pulled my hair into a ponytail, and then lay on the hall rug outside the door.

"The Taylors! *Mom!* The whole family? That wasn't in my head count!" The Ice Princess was losing her cool, but I didn't focus on that. All I could think of was that Emma's whole family might come. And *that* was very interesting.

Emma has three brothers. They've always all been in the background of things—rummaging around their mudroom looking for a lost cleat or watching TV in the living room. They're kind of like furniture. When we talk to them at all, it's just stuff like "Please pass the ketchup" or "Hey! We were watching that!"

Jake is much younger, so he's cute but not exactly a pal of mine, and Matt and Sam are older, so we don't really pay attention to them, and they don't pay much attention to us.

Until recently, that is.

What changed everything was that I had a little direct contact with Matt. He's eighteen months older, but only one school year ahead (he's in eighth grade at Park Street Middle School). Usually I am

4

with Emma when her brothers are around, so I guess I see them from her point of view.

But this time I had to call Matt for help with something for Emma, and it wasn't until he said "Hello" on the phone that in one strange, sudden moment, *everything* changed.

So what happened? First off, I am very efficient. When something needs doing, I just do it. When someone needs calling, I just pick up the phone and dial. And that was what I had done, without even thinking about it.

But Matt's voice sounds much deeper on the phone than it does in person, and when I heard it, it threw me off and I panicked, like, *Who is this person I am talking to?* and *Why did I call him, exactly?* I kind of had an out-of-body experience. I suddenly realized I'd called a boy, and I almost dropped the phone!

But thanks to caller ID he already knew who was calling, so I couldn't exactly hang up. Then, just to confuse me further, in the course of our (very brief) conversation, Matt told me how worried he'd been about Emma, and that he felt bad for some things she was going through at the time.

I was shocked!

I didn't think boys *worried* about anyone! And feeling bad for someone? That is just unheard of! Suddenly Matt seemed like . . . a real *person*. With feelings! In the end, it was I who rushed us off the phone. I suddenly got really, really nervous and couldn't believe I'd had the guts to call Matt in the first place. You know in the old cartoons when the coyote runs off a cliff and his feet are still spinning, but he's in midair and he only falls when he realizes it? That's what happened to me.

And now, when I heard Dylan talking about the Taylors, all I could think of was Matt. And that gave me a funny feeling, like fish were swimming in my stomach.

I hope he comes to Dylan's party, I thought. *Or maybe I don't. Ugh! I don't know what I want!*

Suddenly the door flew open, and Dylan shrieked when she saw me lying on the floor. I blinked as the bright light from her room hit me.

"I hate this family!" Dylan wailed, stepping over me. She stomped down the hall to the bathroom and shut the door as hard as possible without actually slamming it.

"Alexis, honey, what are you doing there?" my mother asked in her "patient" voice.

I rolled up on one side and propped my head on

my fist. "Just interested in the outcome of everything," I replied.

My mother smiled at me and shook her head.

"What?" I said in my most innocent voice. "I
just want to make sure that we get the job."

"You'll get the job, all right, but these better
turn out to be the prettiest and tastiest cupcakes
you've ever baked," Mom said. She's pretty tough.
She's not a CPA and a CFO for nothing.

"Mom, please. We run a very professional
outfit."

Dylan came stomping out of the bathroom and
glared at my mother. "This is the person you'd like
to entrust my dessert to? This . . . worm, lying on
the floor like a two-year-old?"

"That's enough, Dylan. Don't speak like that
about your sister," Mom warned. (She went to
parent training when we were little, and she has all
these certain voices and techniques she uses on us.)

"Yeah," I added. "I'm not two. Or a worm!"

Dylan drew back her leg like she was going to
kick me, and I rolled away and sprang to my feet.

"Girls! Counting to three!" Mom yelled.

Dylan shook her head in disgust and stormed
into her room, where she collapsed dramatically
onto her bed. "The Cake Specialist said they'd even

give me a discount," she muttered. "I would be the first discount they've ever given. They said I drive a hard bargain."

Mom patted Dylan. "I would expect nothing less, darling. But we need to support a business that is in our family. And I know the Cupcake Club will do a wonderful job for you."

"Wonderful!" I repeated, raising my arms in victory.

"Argh!" cried Dylan as she pulled a pillow over her head. "Just leave me alone!" After a moment she added, "And just make sure whatever you Cupcakers propose is in my party's color scheme of—"

My mother and I answered together, "We know, we know, black and gold!"

I put up my hand and my mother gave me a stiff-handed, silent high five. (She's not the high-fiving type).

"I saw that!" accused Dylan from under her pillow.

My mother and I exchanged a guilty smile.

"They'd better be the best black-and-gold cup-cakes you've ever made!" said Dylan. "Or else!"

I rolled my eyes, and we left Dylan to her moping.

"Thanks, Mom," I whispered once we were out

in the hall with Dylan's door safely closed.

"You're welcome, dear," she whispered back. "But you owe me some pretty spectacular cupcakes!"

"Black-and-gold ones! Coming right up!" I said, and we laughed.

We started down the hall. I did a little cha-cha-cha step. I'm obsessed with all the TV dancing shows and like to practice dance moves whenever I can. Music and dance is kind of mathematical, which is why I love it. There's a logical and organized pattern to everything—the chords, notes, and dance steps.

"Is Dylan really mad, do you think?" I asked. All joking aside, I did not want Dylan as my enemy. She is my only sibling, and we are usually pretty good friends.

My mother thought for a moment. "She is getting everything she wants. The place, the music, the food, the date, the decor, the favors. Everything. Now, she is contributing quite a lot of her own money to it, so she does get her say. But I think she can accommodate me on a few extra faces and a special dessert."

"Sounds fair to me," I agreed, and I went to e-mail the Cupcakers with the good news. All we needed was a great idea, one that would keep Dylan from killing me. Oh yeah, and it had to be black and gold!

I just wished I could e-mail them about Matt Taylor being invited to the party. But what would I say?

CHAPTER 2

Earth to Alexis

A couple days later we met at Emma's house. I have always liked baking there because her parents don't mind if things get messy. Mom kind of freaks out when we're baking in her sparkling clean kitchen. (Needless to say, I am not messy, but *some* people can be!) We were just brainstorming that day, but I was still glad to be at the Taylors'. I felt a buzz of nervous happiness and had taken a little extra time laying out my outfit the night before. I told myself it was just because it was a Monday and I wanted to start the week off looking good, but deep down inside I knew the real reason: I might see Matt! Was that weird or what?

Thinking about Matt in this new way was weird too. I wished I could tell someone, but even if I could, I wouldn't know what to say. Was this what a crush felt like? Or was I just being silly? I'm *never* silly!

Meanwhile, Emma and I were in a debate.

"*Please*, Alexis!" Emma was begging, and her big blue eyes widened as she looked at me.

"No," I said firmly, and drew myself up as tall as possible to look like I was in charge.

Mia and Katie were laughing at us as Emma and I argued about whether or not we could use real gold flakes in our proposed cupcake design for Dylan's party. It was true that they would look spectacular, but they were so expensive and, to be honest, I didn't want perfect Dylan to have *real* gold cupcakes! She was being such a brat about everything these days, it would feel like we were rewarding her for her bad behavior.

But of course Emma didn't see it that way as she huffed and crossed her arms. I could see the glimmer of a smile underneath, though, and I smiled at her, narrowed my eyes, and dared her to smile back. Finally she smiled back—victory!

Just then a voice asked, "Hey, what's the deal?" *Matt!*

We hadn't heard him come in and now we all whipped around in surprise. My heart leaped as my stomach got all fluttery again. Matt has light, curly hair and blue eyes, and seemed to look especially cute today.

"Oh, Alexis is just being a tough CFO," said Mia.

"Well, someone has to be, or you'd all just be *giving* these cupcakes away," I said huffily. I wasn't really annoyed, but it made me feel less nervous to act like I was in front of Matt.

"You tell 'em, Alexis!" he said, smiling at me as he went into the kitchen. Was I imagining things or did his eyes twinkle? I was definitely feeling a little light-headed.

Emma grinned. "Huh! Look who's best friends now that you saved my life together," she said, reminding us about the time a few weeks ago when Matt and I worked together to help her out. "Usually he acts like he doesn't even know any of your names!"

Best friends! Hardly, but the idea of Matt and me linked in any way, shape, or form (plus, he'd smiled at me!) caused a warm feeling in my chest that quickly spread up into a blush.

Noticing how red I'd turned, Emma's grin quickly faded, and she gave me a strange look. Uh-oh. I ducked my head down and looked back at my leather-bound account ledger.

"Okay," I said, quickly trying to think of something else. "We have about twenty-five cents per cupcake to work with. Batter is ten cents per cupcake and frosting is five cents, so that leaves us with ten cents for any kind of decoration. By my calculations, the gold costs twenty cents per cupcake and that is just too much!"

"How does she figure this stuff out?" Katie asked the others.

"And why does she *want* to? That's the real question!" said Mia with a laugh.

"Ha-ha. Very funny. *Not*," I protested.

Even though I was talking to my friends, my mind was still on Matt. I heard his footsteps cross the floor above us, and I wondered what he had for homework and what subjects he liked. I also wondered what I would say to make conversation if he came back down. I chewed on my pen cap as I thought.

Suddenly I heard Katie saying, "Earth to Alexis!" and looked up to see everyone staring at me. Apparently Katie had been asking me a question.

I shook my head to clear my thoughts. "Oh, sorry. What?"

"Alexis, did you take your omega-threes today?"

Mia teased. "You seem really spacey!" She always makes fun of me and my vitamins, but I know they work. My whole family is about "optimizing our engines," so we eat superhealthy meals and exercise together, and we like to take supplements.

"Yes, I did," I replied, making a face at her. Usually I don't mind if my friends tease me, but I get annoyed when they make fun of me in front of other people—like Matt. I hoped he couldn't overhear any of this.

"Someone's a little testy!" said Katie as Emma frowned.

"What?" I asked, looking at Emma, and it came out a little harsher than I meant it to.

"Oh, nothing," Emma said, but I knew that wasn't true. Maybe she could tell that her brother was the cause of my freak-out.

Luckily Mia started talking about something else. "Hey, what are you going to wear to Dylan's party?" she asked. Mia is really into fashion, and her mom is a stylist, so clothes are always on her mind.

I was glad for the change of subject, even though it meant we hadn't yet figured out our budget. I told Mia that Dylan was going to set some things aside for me at Icon (Mia and Dylan's favorite store, but not mine), and I could bring the Cupcake Club with me this weekend to go try them on. As long as there wasn't anything too racy, that was good for me. Showing a lot of skin made me nervous. I wished I could get something at Big Blue, which was my favorite store since it was kind of preppy-casual, but they didn't have anything "special" enough for Dylan there. Or anything black and gold enough.

"So we'll go with you before we bake on Saturday, then," offered Katie. "Where are we baking again?"

It should really be my turn, but I didn't say anything for a minute, hoping Emma would offer. I looked down at the ledger.

Mia thought out loud. "Well, today is Emma's, tomorrow is my house, and Friday is Katie's, so . . ."

Everyone was looking at me, so I had to answer. "We could do my place, I guess. It's just that Emma is way closer to the mall . . . if we need to walk."

"Your dad would totally drive us! He's so nice about it!" Katie said. It was true. My dad was willing to drive us anywhere ever since he got his new car.

"I'd much rather be at your house," Emma added. "It's so peaceful and organized and clean! And there aren't any boys. . . ."

Yeah, that's not good news, I said to myself. Inside

16

I felt bummed that we weren't going to be at the Taylors', but I knew it wouldn't be fair not to offer, so I said, "Okay, my house it is."

Then we kept brainstorming and came up with three pretty good ideas for Dylan's party. Well, the other girls did most of the thinking. My mind was upstairs where Matt was the whole time. I kept wondering if and when he was going to appear again. And what I would say to him if he did.

If that afternoon was an equation, it would have looked like this:

$$(Friends + business) / cute\ boy = brain\ dead$$

Here's what we finally came up with:

Option A. Disco cupcakes: white cake with black vanilla frosting and Emma's coveted gold flakes strewn across the top.

Option B. S'mores cupcakes: angel food cake injected with liquid marshmallow and frosted with dark (black-looking) chocolate. They would have a sprinkling of graham crackers on top. They would probably be the best-tasting but not the coolest-looking.

Option C. Gift cupcakes: small yellow cupcakes peeled out of their wrappers and coated with raspberry jam, and then wrapped in a round sheet of black fondant tucked under at the bottom so they looked like a smooth hill. They would be individually wrapped like a gift with gold ribbon tied in a big bow on top. They would definitely be the prettiest ones.

It was a good day's work, though I hardly remember what was said after Matt showed up. Thank goodness I take good notes!

Unfortunately, Matt never came back down before we had to leave. I was tempted to call up the stairs to say bye to him, but that would have been truly weird. I did whisper it as I walked down their driveway, though. No one heard me, so why not?

CHAPTER 3

Project M. T.

My desk is my command center, and I take pride in keeping it superorganized. There are little drawers with all my supplies in tidy little boxes and packages. My pencil cup holds only Ticonderoga #2 pencils, all sharpened, points up, and my pen cup holds only blue erasable FriXion pens. I have a small container of white erasers (the best kind), and then there are my tools: very sharp Fiskars scissors for projects, a flat tin of rainbow-hued watercolor pencils (for graphs and pie charts), an electric pencil sharpener, a three-ring hole punch, a heavy Swingline stapler, and an old-fashioned Scotch tape dispenser.

My family shops the Staples sales religiously, and we are good with coupons and points and our club card. My parents figure that homework time spent looking for supplies is homework time wasted, so they like us to be well-stocked. When we run low on something, we just leave it on the kitchen island and our mom has her assistant reorder it immediately, putting it on her personal account. It's that easy, as they say on TV.

That night, though, despite my desk being fully stocked with supplies, my mind kept drifting away from my homework. It was really infuriating because I hate being unproductive. I had to admit that it was Matt who was distracting me. I was wondering if this was a crush. And if it was, what did I want to come of it?

Did I want him to be my *boyfriend*?

I wasn't sure, but I had to say *not really*. And to be absolutely honest, the idea of having a boyfriend kind of terrified me.

Well, then, did I want him just as a friend?

I was thinking definitely not just as a friend. Maybe something in between? It was hard to quantify it! My feelings about Matt would not organize themselves, and that was superfrustrating. I had no control whatsoever over anything—whether I'd see him, whether he'd speak to me if I saw him, and what we'd say. I played out all kinds of scenarios in my mind as I sat at my desk, watching my timer tick away the half hour I'd allotted to writing flash cards for my vocab test next Tuesday.

Now I was really frustrated. I sighed loudly, slapped the timer off, shuffled the flash cards into a neat stack, clipped them tightly together with a binder clip, and put them in my English bin on top of the desk. I was at a total loss. I grabbed a fresh sheet of white paper from the stack, and then reached for the calculator. Then I started fooling around with numbers, which *always* relaxes me.

I began scratching figures on the page as I thought. First, if I spend twenty minutes a day thinking about Matt, then that's one hundred and forty minutes a week, or two hours and twenty minutes. If I were working, say, at Big Blue for that long, I'd make twenty-five dollars, before taxes. If I were studying, I'd probably get an A on whatever it was. If I were exercising for those twenty minutes a day, and figured on a five minute warm-up and a five minute cool-down, then that was still ten minutes at my optimum heart rate, which was pretty good.

I rested my cheek on my hand and stared into space. Part of my brain was flashing a warning: "This is not scheduled into your planner for today! You are wasting time!" It was true, but I felt sluggish, like I had no control over myself. I certainly had no control over the object of my interest.

Or did I?

I sat up straight in my chair. That's it! What if I took a mathematical approach to my crush? What if I turned my mini obsession into a mathematically quantifiable experiment? I began brainstorming and scribbling onto my sheet in excitement.

My hypothesis was this: Could a crush be manipulated with results that can be replicated every time? Was there a predictable pattern of stimulus and response that I could plan and follow and chart, perhaps ending up with actual mathematical equations to predict Matt's behavior? In other words, could I come up with the perfect formula (or recipe, ha!) for getting Matt to fall for me?

This would be brilliant, I thought, as the neurons in my brain started firing up. It would also kind of justify any lazy daydreaming about Matt by turning those spacey moments into strategy sessions for my experiment. Let's see, what could I hypothesize and test?

What about wardrobe? I usually wear pants. It's kind of one of my trademarks. They are functional, comfortable, and easy to mix and match. But Dylan always wears skirts, and the boys flock to her. So, I wondered, what if I were to wear a skirt or a dress when I saw Matt? Would he react differently to me? Hmm. I wrote:

Project Matt Taylor

M. T., I thought. *More secretive.*
Then I scribbled:

> Clothing experiment: Does he pay more attention to me if I am wearing pants or a skirt/dress?

I would need to conduct an experiment with each, where I timed the length of our interaction and compared the two figures. That would be easy. I could do it at school.

I chewed on my pen cap. What else could I test? Hair up or down? I almost always wore my hair in a ponytail or headband, but Sydney, the head of the Popular Girls Club in my class, always wore her hair down and boys paid lots of attention to her. Granted, her hair was long and blond and mine was long, frizzy, and red, but I could still do a hairstyle test. That sounded good, so I wrote it down.

Ooh! Another idea: comparing the frequency of who initiated our greeting, like in the hall at school. Sydney was giggly with boys, always starting conversations with them, while I only spoke to them if they spoke to me first. Maybe I could try to switch that up a little.

I decided to track my interactions with Matt (in the hall at school? At Emma's?) and collect the data and assess it. That was good.

This experiment called for a dedicated graph paper notebook, so I pulled one out of a cubbyhole in my desk and smoothed the cover with my hand. I could also write conversation starters in it (I had no idea what to say to him if I did see him), and maybe track things I could research that I know he's interested in, like sports and computer graphics. I was excited. At least now if nothing ever came of my interest in Matt, I wasn't *totally* wasting my time. I was practicing math skills!

Just then there was a knock on the door.

"Come in!" I trilled happily. I am always happiest when I am feeling busy and productive.

Dylan opened the door. "Dinner is in five minutes."

I looked at the clock, which read 6:55. We always eat exactly at seven. "Okay!" I said, still writing in my notebook.

My sister narrowed her eyes and folded her arms. "What are you working on?" she asked suspiciously. I guess it looked like too much fun to be homework. But I suddenly realized I did not want this notebook falling into the wrong hands, so I slammed it shut.

"Oh, just some cupcake ideas," I said casually.

"Stuff for my party?" Dylan asked.

"Not quite. Mostly budget stuff right now." *Please don't let her ask to see it.*

There was a pause before she asked, "When are we having the taste test?"

Okay, good, she didn't ask to see the notebook. "Oh, this Saturday. We're baking here, and then you can try all three of the options in the afternoon."

"But I have cheerleading practice on Saturday!" she said with a pout.

"Well, what time?" I asked patiently, ignoring her whiny voice. Sometimes I wondered who was the older sister!

"Four o'clock!"

"Oh, no prob," I assured her. "We'll be done making the samples by three for sure."

"Yeah, but I can't eat all that sugar and then go out and exercise. That will not work! I'm going to talk to Mom." Dylan immediately turned and walked away, not bothering to close the door. She was determined to make this hard for me.

"Whatever, Dyl pill," I said, annoyed.

"I heard that!" she called from the hallway.

"Good!" I whispered, and turned back to my desk, eager to get back to planning my experiment.

Tomorrow was the first day of Project M. T., and I decided that I would wear a skirt and see what happened. I was already dreading wearing the skirt—and what's more, I dreaded seeing Matt almost as much as I looked forward to it!

Who knew superorganized me could be *so* confused?

CHAPTER 4

Can He See Me Now?

*B*rrring!

The bell rang, and Eddie Rossi slammed his book shut and whipped it into his backpack. I thought this was pretty rude to Mr. Nichols, who was kind of old but not totally boring. *I mean, how badly do you want to get out of here, mister?* I thought.

I stared at Eddie with my most disapproving glare, but he didn't look around. Just sat with his backpack on his back, his hands gripping the edge of his desk, poised to launch out of his seat and out the door. I'm usually not that devious, but for some reason, his attitude really bugged me today. So I raised my hand.

"Yes, Alexis?" asked Mr. Nichols.

"Oh, you forgot to assign the homework," I said,

and it didn't take long for Eddie to react. His head snapped around and he glared at me. I gave him a closed-mouth smile and shrugged. *That's what you get, Mr. Rude,* I thought. *Teachers are people too!*

"Ah, thank you, Alexis," said Mr. Nichols distractedly. "I almost forgot . . ."

On autopilot, I copied down the homework and then packed up my bag. Eddie had already sprung out of the room and down the hall. From the back row I could hear Sydney Whitman and Callie Wilson restart their almost incessant chatter. The day was one long gossipfest for them, about movie stars, kids they went to camp with, kids from school, boys—anyone and anything. And it all sounded so utterly mindless and unproductive.

"Good catch on the homework, Alexis!" said Callie brightly. I looked up at her to see if she was making fun of me. She didn't seem to be.

"Yeah," sneered Sydney. "I'd hate to get out of here without something to keep our skills sharp at home."

Well, Sydney's response wasn't surprising. I ignored her and kept stuffing my books into my bag. My cheeks felt hot, but I willed myself not to blush.

Then she started laughing hysterically as she

sauntered out of the classroom with Callie. The next class shuffled in, and I was going to be late. I had no choice but to fall into step right behind Callie and Sydney. I had worn a skirt today as part of Project M. T., and its unfamiliar swish against my legs made me feel insecure. I had worn my hair up, as usual, as a control, so I could isolate the effect of the skirt.

I wondered if I'd even see Matt, after all this strategizing.

Just ahead of me Sydney said to Callie teasingly, "I wonder if we'll see Mr. Hottie today?"

"Oh, I almost hope not! I look terrible!" moaned Callie, who couldn't have looked more perfect.

"When was the last time you saw him?" asked Sydney.

Callie made a sad face. "Last week. And I used to see him every day at camp! It's so unfair!" she wailed.

"Well, maybe you need to get your hands on a copy of his schedule and just make sure you're putting yourself in the right place at the right time!" said Sydney. "I mean, what are we here for, right?"

Wow, scary! I thought. *Is that what we're here for? To get boys to notice us?* But then I realized Sydney had a point. And if so, maybe I should be listening to these two. They did certainly know how to attract boys' attention.

Suddenly Sydney squealed. "Oh my God! Two o'clock! Two o'clock!"

What? What was happening at two o'clock?

Callie flipped her hair and I could see her straighten her clothes. She grabbed Sydney's arm and linked her hand through it, squeezing tightly. I hate when girls walk together like that—it's so annoying! Anyway, I watched to see what was happening.

And just then, I spotted Matt! My stomach felt like it dropped to the floor, and I was hot and cold all over. I'm pretty sure I had an insta-blush. I looked down at the linoleum tiles, then at the lockers on either side of me, the ceiling, anywhere but toward Matt, who was ahead and to my right, walking with a friend toward me. Should I say hi? What was my plan? Suddenly I couldn't remember what I had planned to do! Why didn't I have my strategy book with me? I stared—past my skirt—at my toes.

"Hey, guys!" Sydney called in a loud, high-pitched voice that was sickeningly sweet in a very fake way.

I looked up to see who she was talking to, and it was Matt and his friend!

Callie was pink and she was grinning from ear to ear. What was going on? In confusion, I looked back and forth between the two pairs of friends.

Matt and his friend smiled at Callie and Sydney and nodded in greeting. Matt's friend said something quietly to Matt and Matt nodded again, laughing.

I opened my mouth to say hi to Matt, but thought better of it. I snapped it shut and put my head back down. I couldn't tell if he had seen me. I wondered if either of the boys was the one that Callie liked from camp, and crossed my fingers that it wasn't Matt. Talk about variables! I definitely didn't factor *that* into my experiment!

Okay, calm down, I told myself. *Deep breaths, Alexis.* This was excellent data to collect. I didn't say hi first and he didn't say hi either. But if I said hi first, he certainly would have said hi back. And, maybe next time, he would say hi first. I mean, maybe he didn't even see me, right? And if he didn't see me, how would he know I was wearing a skirt?

How utterly humiliating.

Later, at lunch, I tried to casually grill Emma for information on Matt. I wanted to see if I could piece together whether Callie liked him, or the friend he was with in the hall. But I had to do all this without making Emma suspicious—and that was not easy.

I peeled off the top of my yogurt container and as casually as I could, I asked, "What are you guys thinking of for next summer?"

Mia sighed. "I'd really like to do a fashion design camp in the city," she said. "It's almost like summer school. The only problem is that it's expensive and my mom's also not wild about me sitting indoors under fluorescent lights all summer. I think I have Eddie on my side though, so we'll see." Eddie is her stepfather, and he is awesome.

"I think I might go to the camp that my mom went to when she was a girl," Katie said. "You know, the one she went to with Callie's mom?"

Bingo! "Oh," I said. "Is that the camp where Callie went last summer?"

Katie nodded as she unwrapped her sandwich. "It's supposed to be really fun."

"Right, I was at the same camp," I reminded her. "It was fun. You got to try all different kinds of sports and activities."

Emma nodded, swallowing a gulp of chocolate milk. "Matt went last year too, and he loved it. He was a lifeguard so it was, like, half-price."

What? Matt was at the same camp as me last

summer? Why didn't I remember this? I sputtered and almost choked.

"Whoa! Hands up in the air!" said Mia, patting my back.

Mortified, I looked around the lunchroom to make sure no one else had seen me. I coughed and cleared my throat.

"That's cool," I said in a froggy voice. "Did he . . . *ahem!*" I cleared my throat again. "Did he go with friends?" I asked as innocently as possible.

Emma looked quizzically at me, then slowly said, "Why, yes. He went with Joe Fraser."

"Oh!" I nodded and quickly looked down, pretending to scrape the bottom of my yogurt cup. So there was hope! Maybe that guy today was Joe Fraser! "Anyway, maybe you'll be in my bunk," I suggested to Katie.

"That would be great!" said Katie enthusiastically.

Emma was still looking at me, so I shrugged and added, "Or maybe I'll go to math camp . . . or this cool business camp I read about."

Katie looked puzzled, but didn't say anything.

"Oh, Alexis!" said Mia playfully. "Leave it to you to find a business camp for kids!"

"Speaking of which, are we meeting today?"

Emma asked, finally turning her attention away from me. Whew! There would be no more fishing for information about Matt today. Emma was definitely suspicious, and I knew in my heart of hearts that it would not be a good thing for Emma to find out that I had—yes, I had to admit it to myself after today's noninteraction in the hall—a *major* crush on her brother.

"Oh! It's supposed to be at my house, but my mom asked if we could move it because she's having a dinner party tonight," said Mia. "She doesn't want the kitchen all messed up. I'm so sorry!"

Katie spoke up. "We can't do it at my house either because my grandma is visiting and she will, like, take over if we have it there. I love her, but it's just a little annoying."

Here was an opportunity! I had to think fast. "Oh, bummer! I think Dylan has her study group at our house on Tuesdays . . ." I started to say. Didn't she? Yikes. I'd better check or risk getting caught in a lie. We all looked hopefully at Emma.

Emma sighed. "Fine, we can do it at my house again," she said. "I just think it's so boring and gross. I'd so much rather be at someone else's house where it's quiet and clean and private! Anyway, Jake might be there."

Jake was Emma's little brother, and he could be a bit of a bother.

"Thanks, Emma!" I said. I think I sounded a little too gushing, because she gave me another funny look.

"Okay, *not* a big deal," she said.

"Right!" I agreed, trying to stop myself from smiling too broadly. Tonight I might have another Matt encounter.

And then my heart stopped as I spotted Matt walk into the cafeteria with a group of guys. I could feel my face growing warm, so I quickly looked down at my lunch tray, hoping no one noticed. There was no way he'd come over here, I told myself. But if he did . . .

I reached up and pulled the elastic band out of my hair, casually fluffing my hair and rolling the elastic band onto my wrist. If Matt stopped by, he wouldn't see the skirt, but the hair might be quantifiable.

I watched as he went through the line, and half listened to Emma's summer plans. Suddenly Matt gestured to his friends and began making a beeline toward our table! My mind said "Oh no!" and "Oh yes!" at the same time I quickly sat up and tucked a piece of hair behind my ear. My stomach started doing flip-flops—and then he was next to me!

"Hey, guys," he said.

"Hi," I squeaked. He looked down and smiled!

"Emma," he continued, "Mom asked me to watch Jake on Thursday night, but I just got assigned a group project due Friday. Any chance you can watch Jake and I'll owe you?"

Emma frowned. "I guess so. But it has to be a date of my choice!"

"Fine. Thanks!" he said, and ruffled her hair before taking off.

Emma rolled her eyes. "Brothers," she muttered.

I was thrilled! He had acknowledged me! He had said hi first (sort of!). I couldn't wait to get home and log all this info into my notebook: Score one for "hair down," and none for "skirts." (Whew!)

Now I just had to wait and see if Matt would be at home later today.

CHAPTER 5

Collecting Data

We all arrived at Emma's after school only to find that it was definitely not an option to hold a club meeting there. Emma's mom was having coffee with a friend, and Jake had three little friends over. They had turned the kitchen into a "goo factory," where they were experimenting with every kind of oobleck and gunk that could be created from basic household ingredients.

4 little boys + gooey gunk = total mess

What was amazing was that Emma's mom didn't seem bothered by the mess. My mother would have needed serious CPR if that was going on in her kitchen!

But Emma wasn't pleased.

After I said a quick hi to Emma's mom, I casually (as casually as I could) walked out to the TV room, but no one was there. I went back to the mudroom to Matt's locker (the Taylors all had lockers to hold their gear), and I saw that it was empty. I sighed heavily.

Emma narrowed her eyes at me when I returned. "Did you lose something?" she asked, almost in an accusing tone.

"What? Oh. No . . . no. What?" I stammered awkwardly. "Hey, uh, we can go to my house instead. It's okay," I offered.

Emma was still staring at me.

"I thought Dylan had her study group there?" asked Mia. Mia kind of worshipped Dylan so she filed away every tidbit I said about her.

I shrugged. "Well, maybe they can sit in the den," I said, then heard Emma mutter something under her breath.

"What?" I asked. "Is something the matter?"

Emma looked annoyed. "I don't know why we didn't just go there in the first place," she said.

Now I felt a little annoyed. "It's not exactly ideal

if Dylan's there," I countered. "You know how irritating it is when your siblings are around. It can be really distracting."

"My point exactly," said Emma, looking right at me.

Wait, did she know? But she couldn't. I hadn't done anything to give it away, had I? I shifted uncomfortably and said, "Let's go."

We trudged over to my house. And thankfully (for not making a liar of me) but annoyingly, Dylan was there with her two best friends, Meredith and Skylar.

"Hey, kids," Dylan called out, acting super-friendly for the sake of my friends, I supposed.

"Hi. Are you having your study group here?" I asked.

"Yes," she replied. "We're also working on some new cheer routines."

Have I mentioned that Dylan is maniacal about cheerleading? Maybe more manic about it than about anything else! When she decided she wanted to try out for cheerleading, she was still in eighth grade, but she went to all the practices over at the high school *a year in advance* and videoed them on her Flip. Then she uploaded the videos and studied the routines on her computer and learned them all.

She practiced and stretched and ran and did their whole warm-up routine. And when tryouts started freshman year, they signed her right on. It was like she'd already been doing it for a year anyway. Now she's assistant cheer captain and she's only in tenth grade! Talk about an overachiever. Rah-rah!

"Can we use the kitchen to bake?" I asked. "We have one more test recipe to run through for your party proposal." I knew that if I made it about her, I'd have a better chance at taking over the space.

"Yay! Do we get free samples?" squealed Meredith, who had a major sweet tooth.

I smiled and nodded. You had to love a fan.

Dylan looked at me. I hoped she wasn't going to get all power-trippy on me and say no just for the sake of saying no. Luckily, she simply said, "Just let us finish our drinks, and then we'll move." In our house we aren't allowed to have food or drinks anywhere but the kitchen.

I nodded. That was fair. Maybe the old Dylan was back. She turned back to her friends, and we began dumping our stuff on the couch near the back door.

My ears pricked up when I heard Dylan ask, "So what did he say next?" I glanced back at them. Were they talking about boys?

Meredith smiled shyly in response. "He said he'd like to see me again!"

It sounded like I might get useful info from listening in. Just as I was turning my head to hear their conversation better, Katie asked, "Want to go watch TV? Maybe I can find a *Dancing with the Stars* rerun."

Besides the fact that I live for TV dancing shows, I normally would have said yes just to get away from Dylan and her posse. But today I really wanted to hear what they were discussing.

"Um, you guys go ahead," I said. "I'll just get some stuff set up in here first so we're all ready to go when they're done." I was determined to get as much info as I could from these veterans of the romance trenches.

"Do you need help?" Mia asked sweetly. But that was the last thing I wanted right now! Even though it was Mia, I didn't want to have to make conversation and not be able to pay attention to what Dylan and her friends were saying.

"No," I said more forcefully than I meant to. "Thanks," I corrected myself. "I'm good."

I watched as Mia and the others exchanged looks, then shrugged their shoulders before heading to the den.

I turned back to hear what Dylan and her friends were discussing, only to hear Emma ask me, "Do you have a copy of *Jane Eyre* here? I'm supposed to read two chapters for homework, but I left my copy at home."

Sigh. I love my friends, but they were really bothersome right now! "Sure," I said without even looking at Emma. "Upstairs on my desk."

With my ears tuned to my sister and her friends, I quickly busied myself with measuring out ingredients. The Cupcake Club buys in bulk at a warehouse club and then we divvy up the supplies between our houses. My house, though, holds the bulk of the stuff since I'm in charge of purchasing. I also set out our supplies and preheated the oven.

Room-temperature
ingredients x 5 minutes
of mixing with paddle
attachment = light cupcakes

I made sure everything was neatly aligned on the counter: mixing bowls, measuring spoons and cups, rubber scraper, stand mixer, and timer. I adore the order and mathematics of baking: Add this amount of something plus this amount of something else, cook at this temperature, and you will get this—every time! Now if I could just get the right recipe for Matt + Alexis! I laughed at the thought.

As I took stuff out of the cupboards, I tried to figure out what Dylan and her friends were talking about. Apparently there was an upperclassman Meredith had met at the library where she worked after school, and things were "getting hot" between them. Usually I would have found this kind of talk really boring and a waste of time, but today I felt differently. It looked like I could get a lot of useful info from them.

I quietly moved closer to the table, trying not to miss a word.

"So I wore the sweater you suggested," Meredith told Skylar.

Skylar nodded. "Good," she said. "And?"

"Well, it looked good, and like you said, it's very . . . soft and fluffy, and it's a girlie color. I guess guys really do like that stuff because he did touch my arm when we were talking, like he wanted to feel the material."

"And the perfume?" asked Dylan.

"Yes," said Meredith. "I did just what you said. I wore that vanilla spice from Bath and Body Works. I felt like a doughnut! But I noticed him kind of sniffing the air—in a good way!—when I bent over to stack some books on the cart."

"Well, I told you about the study! Men love vanilla and pumpkin pie above all other scents! It has been tested!" Dylan said, laughing. I was surprised. Boys love Dylan, but I never thought it was something she put any thought or effort into!

"They're all just little boys at heart. They want baked goods and fuzzy things!" Dylan added. She sounded so mature saying that, like she had done it all. She did have a lot of boy friends, but Mom and Dad had just started letting her go out on dates this year. I knew Skylar had a boyfriend over the summer, but I didn't think he was still in the picture. I remembered hearing about some breakup story, but that was way before I was interested in that kind of thing. Like, more than a week ago.

Okay, I thought, the baked goods part sounded easy, especially for me: smelling like them, providing them, describing them in tantalizing detail. No problem! Next I mentally raked through my closet. I didn't really own anything that could be described as fuzzy. I definitely had to do something about that.

My data collecting was going so well that I grew a little bolder. I jumped up to sit on the kitchen island to make sure I didn't miss a word they were saying. I couldn't tell if they noticed me and were ignoring me, or noticed me and were kind of putting on a show for me, or if they just didn't notice me at all (most likely). I waited for Dylan to order me to leave while they finished their drinks. But she didn't.

"And how about your hair?" Skylar asked Meredith. "Was it 'touchable'?" She made quotation marks in the air with her fingers.

Meredith nodded. "I didn't blow it out that day. I set it in rollers, just like we discussed, so it was all springy and curly. He said that it looked different and he actually told me he liked it!" She blushed. "So getting up extra early was worth it!"

"Good." Dylan nodded. "The *Seventeen* survey said that men prefer wavy or loosely curly hair above all else." Boy, I had no idea my sister knew so much about this stuff!

I started thinking about curls. I have a little pack of rag curlers my grandma gave me one Christmas when I was in a *Little House on the Prairie* phase. I had wanted to create curls the way the Ingalls girls did. I could find those and see if they still worked!

I wished I had my notebook so I could write all this stuff down. I tried to visualize equations in my mind to help me remember what the older girls were saying:

Fuzzy texture + girlie color = boy touching your arm

Loopy curls - straight hair = compliment

Food scents / vanilla + pumpkin = boys sniffing

I was intrigued by the studies the girls were saying they had read about boys and what they liked. I had no idea that actual research dollars were being spent on this kind of thing! But now that I thought about it, it made sense. For instance, perfume companies spend a fortune developing perfumes that are supposed to make men fall all over the women who wear them (if you believe the ads). So why wouldn't they put lots of dollars into researching which smells men like best? And shampoo companies of course research what kind of hair men like best. Then they release that information right at the same time they're releasing the new products that make women's hair do just that! I liked figuring out businessy things like this. When things fit neatly into place, it makes me very, very happy. But I also liked the fact that people—scientists, even!—were spending valuable time and money on just the kinds of experiments I was conducting myself. It made what I was doing seem worthwhile.

But more important, I couldn't believe that I'd never paid any attention to the magazines and websites that Dylan and her friends liked to read. It was crazy to think that they were chock-full of all this scientific information about attracting boys, and I'd never known it! Well, I made a mental note to borrow some magazines from Dylan and go online as soon as I could.

Just then Emma came back into the kitchen holding my copy of *Jane Eyre*. She also had a funny look on her face. But I didn't want her interrupting my fascinating information session, so I kind of ignored her. But she just kept standing there, like she wanted to say something to me.

"What?" I finally whispered.

Emma looked at Dylan and her friends, then she shrugged and turned to go back to the TV room. *Whatever,* I thought, and sighed loudly.

Dylan turned to me. "Is that really a hint?" she snapped.

47

"What?" I was alarmed. I wasn't trying to get rid of them! "Oh, no, not at all!" I said quickly. "Take your time. I wasn't rushing you. . . ." My fear must've been obviously genuine, because Dylan's face softened.

"We're ready, actually," she said. "Come on, girls. Let's go outside for a few minutes to work on cheering before we start the chem review."

Meredith and Skylar gathered their mugs and things and, still chatting, went out to the yard. I wish I could have gone with them. I had really gotten some good intel, but it only left me hungry for more.

Then Emma and Katie wandered in. "Ready?" they asked.

"I guess," I said, then realized how I sounded. What was I thinking? We were here to work on our business! We were here to make money! Why was I moping about some boy and filling my head with silly tricks and tips? This was so not me at all! "I mean, yes, I'm ready!" I said brightly. "Let's make some money!"

"Well, all righty then!" said Katie. And we eagerly set to work.

It wasn't until I got upstairs after everyone left that I found my Project M. T. notebook on top of my desk. I had forgotten to put it away last night, not thinking anyone would see it. My heart raced as I thought about Emma. She must have seen it; that's why she gave me that look.

I flipped through it. Luckily, I never mentioned Matt's name. I only called him "The Crush." I actually shivered in relief, but that was a close call. And now I'd have some sort of explaining to do with Emma if it came up (I certainly wasn't going to bring it up myself). I picked up the notebook and looked around the room. Everything in my room was as neat as a pin. All except one place.

I lifted a key out of my desk drawer and used it to open the top drawer in my antique wood dresser. It is a wide and deep drawer, and inside is total chaos. It's the only place in my world that's not organized . . . well, until now with this Matt thing. My messy drawer is where I stash makeup, cheap trinkets, sunglasses, and old candy. I dropped the notebook in and shoved the drawer closed, then relocked it. I was probably too late, but better late than never (which is definitely *not* one of my mottoes).

CHAPTER 6

Mall Madness

The music they play at Icon is so, so loud, and the air freshener or incense or whatever they use to scent the store makes me gasp for clean air. Plus, it's dark. I mean almost pitch-dark. It is not a place I like to spend any time. But there I was on Saturday, with all the Cupcakers (including Emma, who was being a little weird), looking at the dresses that Dylan had placed on hold for me as "pre-approved" attire for her party.

I couldn't believe it. All three of the dresses she chose matched her party decor: black and gold. Was she trying to tell me that I was simply part of the decor? Whatever it was, I was annoyed. Black is really not my color. I don't think it makes me stand out, and I would like to stand out a little—especially if Matt might be there.

Most of all it just got on my nerves that Dylan felt she could pick what I wore. As if otherwise I would wear something that would embarrass her.

Katie scrunched into the corner of the dressing room. "Can you make some room, please?" she shouted over the music. I don't think Mia could hear her, even though she was wedged right up against her. The attendant had warned us we wouldn't all fit, but we had insisted. I didn't want to do this alone.

The room was so tight that Emma was basically sitting on Mia's lap. I was in a corner, trying to pull the first dress over my head.

"What do you think?" I asked after I finally— after struggling for five minutes—got the dress on.

"What?" shouted Mia.

I sighed. Talking was pointless. I jerked my thumb at the door and then went out into the communal viewing area, which was packed with other girls. We waited our turn in front of the only mirror. Finally we got a spot with a spotlight right above it. At least I could now see myself!

I tipped my head to the side and looked at the dress. It was horrible, all black and droopy. Not my style at all.

"It's fine," I said with a shrug, "if lumpy is the look I'm going for."

"What?" yelled Emma.

"Never mind!" I shouted, then looked at the price tag. "Really never mind!" I added, though no one could hear me.

Katie, Emma, and I went back into the dressing room, but Mia decided to wait outside for my "reveal." I looked at the other two dresses. One was short and flouncy. It had a black tulle skirt and a gold bodice. It was kind of prom dressish. The other one was strapless (nightmare!) and long, with a slit up one whole leg. I couldn't imagine my mother approving that one, but it was the kind of dress that a guy might like to see a girl in. Hmm. That would be my next choice. I grunted my way out of the first dress and slid the leg-slit dress over my head. It was no more than a thin piece of satin, with some gold details at the top in a kind of bandeau bathing suit style. Luckily, because it was so slinky, it slid down easily.

I went back out to look at the dress, then gasped when I saw myself in the mirror. Mia, Katie, and

Emma gasped too. I looked like I was twenty-five years old!

"Wow! You're a hottie!" yelled Katie.

"Yeah, you just need to take off the socks!" Emma said in my ear. I looked down. I had on fuzzy pink crew socks. That part did not look so good, but the rest of me screamed *Dancing with the Stars*!

Mia was nodding, but she had her head tipped to the side. "You look amazing, but you do not look like Alexis Becker." She reached over to a dress hanging on a hook. "Here, I grabbed this from a girl who was going to put it back. Try it."

I looked at the dress in her hand. It was not black. It was not gold. It was not too mature. It was a deep raspberry pink V-neck sweater dress—fuzzy and touchable!

"Look," said Mia. "It has slits up each side to make it dressier, and you'd wear it with pale or gold heels, a gold belt—maybe a chain, even— and a great-looking chunky necklace. Go on! Try it!"

I took the dress from her and went back in alone. Seconds later I was out again and staring in the mirror. The color looked amazing on me. The fabric felt amazing. I really, really loved it!

Suddenly someone tapped me on my shoulder.

I turned around and it was Meredith, with Skylar.

"Hi, Alexis!" they yelled, waving.

"You look awesome!" said Meredith.

Skylar nodded. "If you don't get that, I'd love to try it on!" she said in my ear.

I smiled. "Sorry, but I am getting it!" I replied. "Even though it's not black and gold!"

"I can't hear you!" Skylar shouted, giving me two thumbs-up. "But you look great!" she yelled.

I suddenly felt warm and happy, even though I was a little nervous about what Dylan would say. But I decided that she couldn't control everything!

On my way to pay with the money Mom had given me, I looked around—and spotted the only other nonblack clothing in the store. It was a really nice ice-blue long-sleeved V-neck shirt. And it was marked down from $40 to $19.99! I held the shirt up in front of me. It was my size. And I did have enough cupcake money saved up. I decided I couldn't pass up this great bargain, so I looped it over my arm and walked toward the long line at the cash registers.

"We'll wait for you outside!" called Katie.

I nodded and waved to her. As the line snaked around, I looked at what other people were buying. I couldn't believe how many people liked dressing all in black, and they weren't all Goth girls! Icon clearly knew what they were doing and how much people like buying cheap black clothes in a dark, loud, and stinky store.

I stood in line and found myself right behind Sydney and Callie. Before I could decide what to do, Callie said hi. She's kind of nice. I think if Sydney wasn't around to boss her, and Katie was okay with it, she might even be good in the Cupcake Club, but that just won't happen. I just hoped she liked Joe Fraser and not Matt Taylor. I didn't think I could compete with her.

I looked at Sydney, but she ignored me and talked away on her phone.

Callie pointed at my clothes and said, "Those look nice."

I wasn't sure if she was being serious or ragging on me, so I simply shrugged. But it seemed like she was really interested in talking to me, so I asked, "What are you getting?"

She held up a silky black dress with gold detailing—it was my *Dancing with the Stars* dress!

I smiled. "Wow! That is some dress!" *For a grown-up,* I wanted to add.

Callie giggled. "I don't even have anywhere to wear it, but the price is good and when I tried it

on, it looked"—her voice dropped to a whisper—
"amazing, if I do say so myself!"

"Yes, it would look great on you," I said, trying
to be nice. *Just don't wear it in front of Matt Taylor,* I
added silently.

Just then the line began to move, and Sydney
hung up her phone.

"See you later!" said Callie.

I waved and turned away, then looked back
to see Sydney grab Callie's elbow and whisper
something in her ear. Callie looked at me guiltily
and then at Sydney. She shrugged but her smile
faded. Sydney probably yelled at her for talking
to me. *Whatever,* I told myself. But I did feel bad
for Callie.

After I paid I caught up with the others outside
the store.

"Do we need to go meet your dad now or do
we have time to go look at stuff at Claire's?" asked
Mia. "They have some chunky necklaces that would
look pretty with your dress. Then we still need to
find a gold belt and some gold shoes." She thought
for a moment, then added, "Kitten heels, I think."

"Let's go meet my dad," I replied. "I can't spend
any more money! I'd rather be making money!"

"We know!" said Emma, and we all laughed.

I was just about to tell them about Sydney and Callie when who should come around the corner in front of us but Matt and his friend (was that Joe?)! I froze. How did I look? Was I wearing anything touchable? Pink? How was my hair? Did I smell good? What would I say?

"Hey," said Matt. "What's so funny?" (Ooh, score one for Matt saying hi first! Even though it was to all of us, it still counted! I would need to write that down in my notebook.)

"Hey," Emma replied. "Oh, we were just laughing about Alexis."

"Tsk, tsk, tsk, Alexis! Always making the crowd laugh," Matt said with a wink at me. I almost died! But I wished Emma hadn't said that they were laughing me. What was I? Some kind of clown? Hmm. Okay, maybe it was all right if he thought I was funny. I mean, funny isn't bad, is it? Anyway, I was happy just to hear him say my name. I giggled and nervously looked around.

Then I caught Emma's eye. And I could tell that she knew. Cripes. What was I going to do now? I looked down at my shoes, which were my dorky-looking Merrells. I would absolutely have to ditch them forever when I got home. I looked up again and willed myself to say something, anything, when suddenly someone called out, "Hey, boys!"

Ugh! Sydney! She and Callie walked up to our group, but their eyes were only on the boys.

Matt turned around. "Oh, hey," he said very casually. I caught his friend looking over at Mia (what is that all about?) and then at Callie and Sydney. Ignoring the rest of us, Sydney linked her arm through Matt's and gave it a squeeze. I started to tense up.

"What are you boys up to?" Sydney asked in a very flirty way, flipping her hair from one side to the other. "Have you eaten lunch yet?"

"What? Oh." Matt looked unsure. "Not yet. Have you guys?" he asked us.

Opportunity knocking! I started to shake my head no, but Emma spoke up. "No. We were just leaving. See ya!"

And she started walking away! Mia and Katie followed her, but I was stuck in my spot. *Wait!* I wanted to yell. *Let's stay! Let's have lunch with them!* Joe seemed to feel the same way because he looked disappointed as Mia walked away.

Sydney was now sort of pushing Callie at Matt, and they were both looking embarrassed.

"Bye!" Matt called to us.

"Later," I said in as casual a tone as possible. I

turned to go with my friends, and I was trying my best to look like I didn't care at all that I just lost out on a chance to have lunch with Matt.

We rode the escalator down in silence to meet my dad in the parking area. I hated Sydney, but that was nothing new. I also kind of hated Matt now. And Emma. Why couldn't she have said, "Oh, sorry, Sydney Horrible Whitman, but we are all going back to my house with my cute brother and his cute friend and we are going to hang out all day and play Wii and you are so not invited." *Why couldn't she have done that?*

Outside my dad waved from his spot in the pickup area. He looked so happy to see us that I felt a tiny bit better.

What cheered me up more was when he said, "Want to go to Harrison's for lunch?"

Harrison's Roast Beef is my absolute favorite lunch place in the whole world. It would be hard to stay upset if I was going there. Plus, if we all went to lunch together, it meant Emma would not catch me alone and have a chance to grill me about what she found out today.

So I called back, "You betcha!" to my dad, and we all hurried to the car.

I'll have another chance to say hi to Matt again soon,

I told myself. *And maybe I'll be dressed better then, anyway,* I thought, looking at my boring outfit. Maybe it was a good thing this happened. This way I could keep up a mysterious air and let Matt think I'm really funny without me having to actually prove it. ("Better to remain silent and be thought a fool than to open your mouth and remove all doubt." That quote is one of my mottoes.)

CHAPTER 7

My Sister Really Takes the Cake!

During lunch at Harrison's my father and I told the Cupcakers about the dance we were planning for Dylan's party. We had been practicing most nights after I finished my homework.

"You have to see how graceful Alexis is!" my father bragged. "She can really cut a rug." He nodded proudly. Some people might say he is a total nerd, but I love him.

"Oh, *Dad*!" I said, like I was embarrassed, but I wasn't really. Our dance was the one thing that I was feeling really good about, as it took me away from all the crazy feelings that were going through my head: my dislike of Sydney, my crush on Matt, my frustration with Emma, the nervousness I was feeling about Dylan and the cupcakes we were about to present to her.

We had a great time at Harrison's. Dad kept us laughing with his corny jokes.

When we got home, Dylan and Mom were at the kitchen table, addressing the last of the party invitations on black envelopes with gold gel pens.

"Hello, Mom! Hello, Dylan!" I called as we walked in.

Dylan nodded at us without saying a word before going back to writing. The scent of the pens was so strong that I could feel it going to my head and making me a little light-headed. I was dying to see if Dylan had addressed the invitation for the Taylors yet; I wouldn't believe Matt was actually invited until I saw it in black and . . . gold. I craned my neck to see where she was on her list (created as an Excel spreadsheet on the computer, of course).

Dylan looked at me. "What?" she demanded.

"Oh, nothing!" I replied, waving my hand, and got ready to start baking.

"Just get going on the cupcakes, because I have to leave for practice at three thirty, and an athlete can't practice on a system filled with sugar."

"Ah, don't worry, we'll be done in plenty of time," I said, smiling at my friends.

Just then Mom asked, "So how did the dress turn out, Alexis?"

I could feel my face grow instantly hot. Should I make up a fib?

"Oh, you know . . ." I was stalling for time, but Katie cut in.

"Oh, Mrs. Becker, you have to see the dress that Alexis bought! It looks so beautiful on her!"

I glared at Katie and elbowed her. Poor Katie looked at me in pain and surprise. Luckily my mother was looking down, so she didn't see this exchange.

What? Katie mouthed at me. I shook my head vigorously, but they had already heard Katie.

"Are you going to show us the dress?" asked Dylan.

"Not right now," I said briskly. "Let's get the cupcake samples ready, and then I'll model it if you have time before practice." This made sense to Mom and Dylan, so they both nodded and went back to what they were doing. Now I could focus on the cupcakes! I would deal with what was sure to be a dress crisis later.

Without any more interruptions, my friends and I were able to work quickly to turn out samples for three different cupcakes: the disco, s'mores, and the gift one. Much as I hated to admit it, Emma had been right about the gold flakes. They looked magical and I knew Dylan would totally go for them. The s'mores were tasty but not elegant, just as we had suspected, and my little gift idea looked great, but not very appealing.

We stood holding our breath as Dylan and my parents inspected our treats.

"Oh, girls, these are lovely!" Mom said.

"I'll take them all," said Dad as he playfully lifted the platter, pretending that he was going to run off with it.

"Dad!" I called out just as Dylan took the plate away from him. Suddenly everyone was really quiet and serious as Dylan examined the cupcakes from all angles, tilting her head this way and that like a judge on a cooking show.

"Oh, Dylan, come on!" I said. My sister could be so exasperating!

But Mia grabbed my arm and whispered, "The customer is always right." Since that is one of my own mottoes, I didn't say anything else. I set my mouth in a firm line to keep it shut and crossed my arms in front of me.

Then Dylan leaned over the platter and smelled the cupcakes. I was about to have another outburst, but my mom shot me a look. What was wrong with Dylan? Why couldn't she say "Wow" or "Hmm . . . not what I want," like normal people would?

After what felt like several long minutes of sniffing, Dylan asked, "Do you have a knife?"

I groaned. I couldn't believe she asked for a knife! We were at home, and Dylan knew very well where the knives were. I was just about to say something when Mia replied cheerily, "Yes, we do!"

She picked one from the butcher block and handed it to Dylan with a flourish. Dylan cut each cupcake in half, and then in quarters. They looked really awful all splayed out like that.

"Dylan, honey, what are you doing?" Mom asked.

"I want to see what they look like inside," Dylan answered. "Then I'm going to taste them, but it's not like I'm going to eat an entire cupcake of each!"

"Well, I'd love to try one—a whole one," Dad said. "I've been waiting long enough. Do I have your permission, your highness?" He looked at me and the other Cupcakers and wiggled his eyebrows.

Dylan rolled her eyes. "Okay, let's sample."

My father took a s'mores cupcake, which he'd been eyeing the entire time, and took a huge bite.

"I'm not usually a fan of marshmallows, but this is dynamite!" he said. "I vote for this one."

My mother also picked the s'mores cupcake, and agreed with him. "Oh, the cake alone is so wonderful, but the marshmallows and the cracker crumbs make this absolutely delicious!"

I smiled. I knew those would be the tastiest.

Dylan took a bite of a sliver of the gold flake cake. She chewed it thoughtfully as we waited for her comment. When she put down the rest of her sliver, Emma asked anxiously, "Is it not good?"

"Oh, no, it's fine. I'm just not a big dessert person," said Dylan with a shrug. Argh! I wanted to scream. Poor Emma looked disappointed.

Next Dylan tried the gift cake. She pinched off a bit of the fondant and nibbled on it. Then she took a tiny bite. She bobbed her head from side to side as she chewed, as if she was weighing it against the previous cupcake. Finally she swallowed and turned toward the cabinet.

"Well?" I asked.

Without answering me, Dylan took her time getting a glass and filling it with water. Then she held one finger up while she drank and we all waited.

"Fine," she said finally.

"Fine?" I asked, annoyed. "What does 'fine' mean? Do you like it or not?"

"Dylan, try the s'mores one. You will love it," said my father.

"Okay, okay," she said, like she was doing us a huge favor. As with the other samples, Dylan took a small bite, and we all watched as she chewed. Now, I spend a lot of time around people eating cupcakes, and I know what I see. I could tell that Dylan *loved* that cupcake! Her features softened, her eyes lit up, and her mouth lingered over the bite before swallowing it. I'm sure I even saw a slight smile on her face when she was done.

"So?" My mom asked, as sure as we were that Dylan's choice would be the same as hers and Dad's.

Somehow the Dylan who enjoyed that very delicious s'mores cupcake two seconds ago was able shake her head and look sympathetic. "I am so sorry, kids, but none of these is right for my party," she said.

There was silence for a moment. We were all stunned, even my parents.

"Wh-wh-what?" I stammered. "What do you mean? You loved that last one! I saw it on your face!"

Dylan shook her head again with a look of

pity. "No, Alexis, the problem is that the tasty one is ugly and the pretty ones aren't very tasty." She shrugged. "Back to the drawing board?"

"Argh!" I screamed.

"Girls, girls, you all did a wonderful job. Dylan, how about a thank-you, first of all, to the Cupcake Club," instructed my mother. I could tell she was mad.

"Thank you," Dylan muttered without looking at us.

My friends were all standing there, not sure what to say. I was mortified. Who was this mean girl and what had she done with my sister, Dylan?

My mom took Dylan by the arm and led her out of the kitchen, which was a good thing, for Dylan's own safety.

"Well, I loved them!" Dad said enthusiastically. "How could anyone possibly choose? Now, let's see, if I was having a birthday . . ." He was clearly trying to make us feel better, but it was not helping.

"It's okay, Dad. We'll just clean up," I said, gently shooing him out.

Later, as I was washing off the frosting bowl, thinking about how mean and ungrateful Dylan was, my party dress popped back into my mind. *Ha!* I thought. *I'm glad I got a pink dress! Why should I have to go along with everything Dylan says and wants, anyway? I'm sick of having to do everything she says.* Now, instead of dreading what she would say about my dress, I couldn't wait to see her face when I put it on!

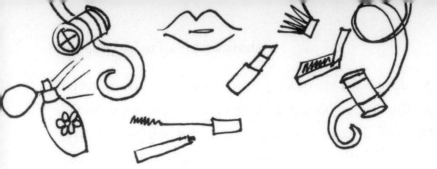

CHAPTER 8

Hello, New Me!

Right before Dylan left for cheerleading practice, she sent out an e-mail my mother made her write. It was to everyone in the Cupcake Club:

> Dear Cupcake Club,
> Thank u 4 the cupcakes u baked 4 me.
> I'm sorry if I was a difficult customer, LOL.
> I'm sure we will reach an agreement at
> some point.
> Dylan

It felt a little halfhearted, if you ask me. Note that she said "*if* I was a difficult customer" not "*that* I was a difficult customer." That is pure Dylan. Anyway, I figured that my parents are the real clients and

I knew we could find something that would work for everyone. I just felt bad about Emma and her gold flakes, not to mention embarrassed in front of my friends that I had such a jerky sister.

The others were nice about it, though, and in the end we were all laughing. Plus, they got me excited about my dress, and I actually tried it on and modeled it for my parents a few minutes after Dylan had left for practice. My parents loved it, and my mother said, "eh," when I told her that Dylan would probably be really mad. My father twirled me around, and we both decided it was perfect for our dance. I only hoped Matt would like it as much as everyone else did.

My father and I were still twirling, and my friends and mother were talking in the living room, when Dylan suddenly rushed in, breathless. I froze.

"Has anyone seen my other sneaker?" she cried in despair.

Then she saw me and narrowed her eyes. "*What* are you wearing?" she asked.

All the courage I felt before about standing up to her left me. "Um . . . ," I said.

"It's her dress for your party!" Mia sweetly answered.

"Yes, doesn't she look amazing?" Katie added.

71

Oh, great. I braced myself for a big speech from Dylan.

"What?" she shrieked before stamping her foot. "It's pink! This is not one of the dresses that I picked out! You know what the party colors are—"

Before Dylan could launch any more ugly words at me, Mom grabbed her and pulled her out of the room. Again! My friends and Dad and I were all speechless for a minute.

"Whoops," Emma finally said.

"I should not have said anything!" Mia said, looking really upset.

"Don't worry, girls," Dad said, "I apologize for Dylan's rude behavior . . . again. Don't ever turn sixteen!" He left the room to look for Mom and Dylan.

"Wow," I said. "Sorry about that. I guess I knew it would come, sooner or later."

No one knew what else to say, so we stood around awkwardly until Emma suggested that they leave. I hated for my friends to leave on such a sour note, but it was probably a good idea.

As the girls headed out the door, Emma turned to say, "Thank you for a lovely afternoon." And we all started laughing, hard.

"Oh! Don't forget these!" I said, handing each

of them their black-and-gold party invitations. "Dylan can't wait to see you all at her party next month! Just don't forget to wear pink!" This got us all howling again.

"What are we doing tomorrow?" asked Katie once she stopped giggling.

"Is Dylan free?" Mia asked with a straight face, and we all fell down laughing.

When we finally stopped laughing, my friends left, promising to talk again later. I cringed at the thought of them discussing Dylan. Ugh. Emma was lucky she had brothers.

Mean sister + friends
witnessing = total
embarrassment

As mad as I was about Dylan's behavior, I didn't feel like asking Mom what happened when she talked to Dylan. I needed a break from thinking about her. All I could think about was working on Project M. T. But first I had to throw my Merrells to the back of my closet. "Buh-bye," I whispered. "See you guys some time after never."

Then I opened my locked drawer and took out my notebook, grabbing some forbidden SweeTarts along with it. I sat at my desk and first logged in my most recent encounters with Matt, noting who said hi first and (possibly) why. Then I turned on my computer and googled some studies about how to attract boys.

I found out some crazy stuff! Like girls care more about boy's looks than boys care about girl's. And that boys like faces that are symmetrical. That is their main thing, not that they actually realize it. Just the researchers did.

Hmm. I wondered about my face. Do I have a symmetrical face? Doesn't everyone? I mean, I have two eyes, two eyebrows, two nostrils. I stood up and looked at myself in the mirror. I looked pretty symmetrical. But was I really?

I clicked on the lamp and propped my chin on my fists. I wanted to examine myself scientifically. Here's the data I collected: My left eye was a little bigger than my right eye if you looked really closely. Also, my left eyebrow kind of had a pointed arch while my right one was more of a smooth arch. Eek! Was that bad? My nose looked the same on both sides, and my cheeks, ears, whatever. I couldn't tell if one was off.

I went back to the computer. How symmetrical did you have to be? I googled again and learned that on a scale of one to ten, Angelina Jolie is only a 7.67 in symmetry. The researcher said she lost points because of those lips. Gosh. If Angelina wasn't a perfect ten, that was not good news for me. I am no Angelina Jolie, that's for sure.

I read on. Another article said boys liked makeup on girls, but only two kinds: foundation to even out skin tone, and eye makeup, to darken the eyes. My skin is pretty even, but eye makeup was something I could try.

I reached into my top drawer and took out an eye makeup kit that Mia had given me at a sleepover. It had dark shadow, light shadow, medium shadow, eyeliner, and mascara. I had no idea how to use any of them, but how hard could it be? If I needed help, there was a little map in the box that showed how to put it all on.

I suddenly decided I needed a total makeover.

Makeup + hairdo + new outfit = gorgeous and noticeable Alexis!

I grabbed the eye makeup kit, along with the curlers from my grandmother, the new ice-blue shirt, and purple beads I already had, and hustled down the hall into the bathroom. I ran a shower, shampooed my hair, and then, following the directions on the package, I rolled my hair up in the curlers and used a blow-dryer. Next, I put on the blue shirt and beads, and began applying the eye makeup.

I used eyeliner to draw a thick line along my upper and lower lashes, just as I'd seen my old babysitter do when I was younger. I stood back to look at what I'd done. Wow, I looked a lot older! Then I leaned back in and brushed light shadow just below my (asymmetrical) eyebrows and then, following the diagram in the kit, medium shadow in the creases of my eyes, and finally, the darkest shadow along the rim of my lid. Finally, I opened the mascara and brushed my eyelashes to a staggeringly long length.

I stood back again. OMG.

I either looked like a raccoon or a supermodel. I couldn't decide which. I turned my head all the way to the left and looked back at the right side of my face; then I looked back at my left side. I liked the left better. Next, I looked straight at the mirror and sucked in my cheeks, trying to look vampire-ish. Then I tucked my chin under and looked up through my eyelashes. That was the best look, I thought. The only thing ruining it was the curlers. I put my hand to my head and touched them. They were dry. Time for the big reveal!

I loosened the curlers without looking, then I flipped my head down and ruffled my hair with my hands, finally flipping my hair back as I stood up and looked in the mirror.

Uh, wow? I had a huge head full of curls—and it looked ridiculous! Or maybe it looked great? I didn't know! I knew I looked different, that was for sure.

Just then there was a knock at the door. "Alexis, dinner," Dylan called.

Yikes! I had been so busy making myself over that I forgot what time it was.

What do I do now? Wash it all off and pull my hair back into some kooky kind of ponytail? Or go down there as if nothing was different? I didn't want to spill anything on my new shirt, though.

"What's for dinner?" I called back.

"Grilled trout, broccoli rabe, and quinoa," replied Dylan.

It sounded pretty stain-free. And it was only my family. They've seen me at my worst.

So I smiled and winked at myself as I took one

last look in the mirror. Then I gave myself a big spritz of the cinnamon bun perfume that Dylan had on her side of the vanity. Yum! I smelled like . . . the food court at the mall. Oh well.

"Ta-da!" I cried as I flung open the door, but no one was there.

Just then the phone rang. I looked at the caller ID. It was Emma.

"Hey!" I called out, when I picked up the phone.

"Oh, hello, dear. Is that Alexis?"

It was Mrs. Taylor! "Oh, sorry, Mrs. Taylor. I thought you were Emma!" I said, laughing. "Are you calling for my mother?"

"Oh, no, don't bother her. I'm just calling to RSVP to the lovely invitation to Dylan's party! You were so kind to invite us all. We'd love to come."

"W-w-we?" I stammered.

"Yes, Mr. Taylor, Emma, and the boys and I. It sounds like great fun!"

I couldn't believe it! Matt was coming to Dylan's party! I had visions of seeing him at the party, of him seeing me in my new, fuzzy, touchable dress.

"Alexis . . . are you still there?" Mrs. Taylor asked. Oops!

"Oh, yes, I'm sorry," I said. "It's great that all of you can come!"

"Will you tell your mom for me, please?"

"Of course! She'll be so happy. Thank you! Thank you so much!" I gushed.

Mrs. Taylor laughed. "Actually, we thank you! We'll see you soon, dear."

I did a victory dance after we hung up, then ran down the stairs. "Mom!" I yelled. I couldn't wait to share the good news.

CHAPTER 9

The Beckers Try Harder

$\mathcal{M}$om!" I skidded in my sock feet into the kitchen, breathless. "The Taylors can come! All of them!"

"Oh, that's wonderful, honey. Write it down in the RSVP notebook by the phone, then grab a plate," Mom said without looking at me. She seemed extra focused on tossing the salad. "We have a lot to discuss."

I frowned at what she'd said. Her tone told me someone was in trouble, and I knew it was not me.

But Dad did look up and did a double take when he saw the new me. "Whoa, tiger!" he said, laughing.

I wrote the first RSVP on the list and turned to face him. "Hello, Father," I said casually—just as

Dylan walked in and immediately screamed.

"Alexis! What on Earth did you do to yourself?"

At that, Mom finally looked up. "Oh, Alexis!" she exclaimed.

Suddenly I wasn't so sure about my new look. "What? Don't you like it?" I asked (fake) confidently.

Mom came over and lifted a curl. She let it go, and it sprang back against my head. "I love the curls!" she said. "I'm not wild about the makeup, though."

"I'm trying to play up my eyes," I said.

"Well, sister, they are played up, that's for sure," Dylan said with a snicker. Then she peered over my shoulder to look at the RSVP book. "Who called? The Taylors? Already? And they're *all* coming? Ugh! What's that smell? Are we having apple crisp for dessert?"

"It's my perfume," I said stiffly.

"All right, before any of this goes any further, I'd like you to get your food and sit down at the table. We are having a family meeting." My mother was using her firm voice (parenting class), sounding the way she does when I talk to her on the phone while she's at work.

Dylan huffed, but didn't say another word as she

81

sat down. I had to admit I was looking forward to seeing her in the hot seat.

"Girls," my mother began, "we are not acting as a fully functioning family unit. There is discord, agitation, unhappiness, malice, greed, envy, you name it." She looked at both of us until we returned her level gaze. As I was pretty guilt-free, I just sat there, but Dylan did squirm a little.

"Your father and I are disappointed in the turn things have taken. In our family, we do not condone speaking rudely to one another, nor treating one another dismissively or high-handedly, nor do we humiliate one another in public. The Beckers are loyal, supportive, and kind. The Beckers . . ."

"Try harder," I finished. It was our family tagline. Ever since my mom had read *The Seven Secrets of Successful Families*, we had to have a motto as well as other "guiding principles." Never mind that our tagline was the same tagline as some international car rental company.

"Exactly right," Dad said, nodding.

"And there hasn't been enough trying lately," Mom added, looking at me.

I was surprised. Why me? "I have been trying!" I protested. "I made the cupcakes, I went to that smelly clothing store—"

"Okay, Alexis. We know." My mother raised her hand. "Dylan—"

"Oh, it's always me!" Dylan cried. "Why is she never in trouble?"

"Because I'm perfect!" I gloated.

"That's enough, Alexis," Mom warned. "You need to be more gracious. We have seen to your wishes, inviting your friends to the party and hiring you to create the cupcakes—"

"Wait! That's not a done deal!" Dylan yelled.

"Yes, it is," said my father sternly. "And you don't have to yell."

"But they haven't even presented a good option yet—"

"I am sure that they will," Dad replied as Mom nodded in agreement. "The Cupcake Club will be providing the dessert."

Yay!

"That is so unfair!" Dylan said, leaning back and crossing her arms. "It's *my* birthday party! I should—"

"Dylan, listen to me," Dad said. "What is unfair is how you humiliated Alexis in front of her friends today. Twice. You put them through the wringer on timing and color scheme. Then you treated them like peons when you sampled their hard work. You acted like a spoiled brat and were totally ungrateful. These girls all look up to you, and any one of those wonderful cupcakes is worthy of your party. Then you were absolutely horrid about Alexis in her pretty dress. This party-planning has made you high-handed and inconsiderate. We understand that you want it to be a wonderful event, but nothing is perfect. You must understand that people will still like you even if your cupcakes don't look like they were made on TV and your sister doesn't match the color scheme!"

Dylan was looking down. It looked like Dad's words were sinking in.

"The most important thing in life is how we treat people," he continued. "And you have not been treating any of us nicely. So before things get any worse, your mother and I say stop! Stop it right now! And bring back the wonderful daughter we had before all of this started."

I looked sideways at Dylan, but couldn't tell what she was thinking.

A heavy silence hung over the table. Then finally, Dylan said, "I'm sorry," in a very quiet voice. "It's just . . . oh, never mind. I'm just sorry."

My mother came around the table to give her

a hug. She kissed her on the top of her head and said, "We love you, honey. The real Dylan. Not this party-planning nightmare person, do you understand?"

Dylan nodded, tears filling her eyes. My father reached over and took her hand. "We know you want this party to be special, and it will be," he said. "We will all work hard to make it so. You just need to do your part and be gracious. Take a deep breath and know that everything will be fine. Okay?"

Dylan nodded again, then picked up her fork. I think she finally realized how mean she'd been lately. My parents and I chatted about random stuff as we ate, but we all finished quickly. I went upstairs to shower again and get rid of the makeup. Then I changed into my pj's and went back to my room. When I got there, I found Dylan sitting at my desk! My Project M. T. notebook was on the table in front of her and she was staring at me.

"Oh my God," I said.

CHAPTER 10

Is She Really My Sister?

$\mathcal{D}$ylan had the notebook in her hand and started walking around me. "What is this?" she asked in a teasing voice.

I thought I might throw up. I studied Dylan's face to see if I could tell which way this was going to go. Was she going to mock me? Pity me? Blackmail me?

"Um . . . ," I said, stalling for time.

"Are you . . . Do you like someone?" she asked.

I decided to take a breezy, confident tone. "Well, what if I do?" I asked.

"So what is all this . . . math and stuff in here?"

"Oh, just data!" I waved my hand dismissively. The less she thought I cared, the less she would press me. Probably.

"Who is it?" she asked.

I didn't know if the talk at dinner made her turn over a new leaf or if it made her resent me. I wasn't sure I should tell her. What if she ended up using it against me?

"Um . . ."

"You can tell me," she said encouragingly. "I won't say anything." Dylan even looked sincere, so I decided to tell her.

"Um . . . it's Matt." Maybe if I didn't say his last name . . .

"Matt Taylor?" she guessed immediately.

I looked down at my feet and nodded, feeling my cheeks suddenly getting hot.

"He's cute," she said, and for some strange reason I was happy that she "approved" of my choice. "Does he know you like him?" she asked, flipping through the pages.

"No!" I said quickly, horrified by the idea.

"Do you want him to know?"

"What? No way!" I'd rather die.

"So where are you going with all this?"

"I just . . . I just want him to notice me. And like me, I guess." There. I'd said it.

Dylan was quiet for a moment. Then she asked, "Do you want my help?"

I eyed her suspiciously. "What do you mean?" I could just picture her telling Matt flat out that I liked him, and that would be a disaster.

"I know what it's like to have a crush who hardly knows you exist, that's for sure!" Dylan said, laughing.

I paused. Was this a trick?

Dylan continued, "I also know some stuff about boys and what they like. And about how to present yourself." She looked at me critically. "And I do think you're ready for a more mature look. The makeover you did wasn't a bad idea. You just went too far, too fast."

I kept looking at her, not sure if I could really trust my own sister.

"Come on," she said in an encouraging tone. "I owe it to you. Let me try."

"Okay . . . ," I finally agreed. "But in the morning. I can't do it again tonight. I have too much other stuff to do."

"Fine. We'll get up early and do it, okay?"

I nodded, still waiting for this to turn into some sort of prank.

Dylan got up and headed for the door, then turned around. "And Alexis?"

"Yes?"

"I'm sorry."

Wow. An apology from Dylan, and I didn't even have to ask for it!

"For which part?" I asked.

"Everything." And she closed the door.

I sat down and sighed loudly, part of me wondering if I had just imagined the past five minutes. Dylan had really turned around! I started to finish entering the new data and notes on some new techniques, like hair-flipping, arm-grabbing, and lunch-inviting—not that any of them were my style.

I chewed on my pen cap as I asked myself the question Dylan had just asked. What did I want? What was my goal with Matt? Was it that I wanted him to just notice me? He already had. But wanting him to like me back seemed major, and maybe too big of a goal. Like more than I really wanted. I think.

My parents always tell us, when we have a big project due, to break it into smaller, more manageable chunks or goals. So if my big project is for Matt to fall madly in like with me, what would a smaller chunk be?

Chew, chew, chew. I looked at my pen cap. It was totally mangled. I twirled it around, and it looked like it was dancing. And then the answer came to me.

A dance. One wonderful, dreamy dance with Matt. Then he'd see how graceful and talented I was, and I'd have the chance to really charm him.

I smiled just picturing it, like a scene out of a Disney movie: *Cinderella*, *Beauty and the Beast*, *Enchanted*. One dance with the prince, and the rest is history. That was my goal.

Relieved to now have an actual goal, I put the notebook away, then did a huge e-blast to all of the Cupcake Club's previous clients, advertising our new flavors (s'mores being one of them), wrote out forty vocabulary flash cards, did a math crossword puzzle, reorganized my planner, and cleaned up my room.

Later that night, when I went to brush my teeth, I nearly tripped over a pile of teen magazines that Dylan had left outside my door. "Get Him to Notice YOU!," "7 Days to a Brand-New You!," "Flirty Tips & Tricks to Wow Him!" the headlines screamed. Well, I certainly had my work cut out for me.

The next morning Dylan gave me a crash course in flirtation and a real makeover. I think even my parents were happy that we were doing something together and not bickering. It was like when we were little and we used to play Barbie dolls together for hours. My Barbie would run the clothing store and Dylan's Barbie would come in to shop. My Barbie would bargain and haggle and put stuff on sale, and her Barbie would try everything on and leave it in a pile on the dressing room floor.

First Dylan and I looked through the magazines together to find a good new look for me. She talked about what I had heard her discussing with Meredith and Skylar, about pretty colors (no black, gray, or brown), touchable fabrics (fuzzy, floaty, silky, smooth), and patterns (floral is good; plaid, not so much). She went through my closet and also brought out some of her own(!) clothes to put together five new school outfits for me—complete with shoes and accessories!

I have to say, she was really getting into it, and she was being a big help. I think she liked that I was agreeing with everything she said.

Next Dylan made me shave my legs, which was gross and hard and took forever (I cut myself twice), but the result was pretty dramatic. She gave me a mud mask for my face and a quick manicure/ pedicure (just clear nail polish because, she said knowledgably, boys don't like colored or fussy nails). Then she had me wash my hair and deep condition it, and she set it in hot rollers we borrowed from our mother. They were heavy and felt like they were pulling out my hair, but when she took them out, my hair fell in soft waves, like a Disney princess!

Finally she taught me how to put on makeup. "The point," explained Dylan, "is that no one should notice you are wearing makeup. You should look like yourself, only better."

Dylan gave me a tiny hint of pink blush to perk up my face and make me look healthy. (According to Dylan, boys respond to healthy looks. It has to do with the evolution of the species.) Then she gave me a cinnamon-and-ginger-laced pale pink lipstick with what she called "blue undertones" to make my lips plump up and my teeth look even whiter. Finally, she drew the faintest lines with brown eyeliner at only the outer corners of my eyes, and then she curled my eyelashes and lengthened them with a little brown mascara. When she turned me around to face the mirror . . . I loved what I saw! I looked great!

"Wow! Thanks!" I exclaimed. It was me, just a better-looking me!

Dylan smiled proudly at me, her handiwork.

"Now let's talk flirtation," she said. "There are two ways to get guys," she said, holding up two fingers. "You can be a normal girl or a supergirlie girl. The supergirlie girl technique tends to work well on younger guys and dumber guys; guys who don't really understand girls and are too shy to pursue them. The normal girl technique attracts the better guys, but it takes longer. Like sometimes years longer. Do you follow me?"

"Um . . ." I wasn't sure what she was talking about. "Do you mind if we go in my room, so I can write all this down in my notebook?"

Dylan laughed. "Fine, whatever," she said.

I made her wait outside while I took the book out of the drawer. "Okay!" I called, and she came in and continued her lecture. I scribbled madly, happy to have specific directions to follow.

From what Dylan was telling me, it seemed that Sydney and Callie go with the supergirlie girl technique, and I prefer the normal girl way.

The supergirlie girl approach meant you had to be aggressive, giggly, loud, super touchy-feely, overdressed, made-up, and perfumed, and you always traveled in pairs, never alone. Supergirlie girls often act grossed out or incompetent to try to get help from boys, and this would in turn make the boys feel good about themselves. However, the supergirlie girl way could backfire because it makes girls appear so different from boys, and some boys could get scared off. But it often worked because boys are so shy and clueless, especially when they're younger, that the girls just go after them and grab them, and the boys never see it coming. They think girls are supposed to be like that, and they're just happy to not have to do the work of asking girls out and stuff. The supergirlie girl approach was based on the idea that boys and girls are totally different and foreign creatures to each other, and girls had to do a lot of planning to get what they wanted.

Whew! I was so glad that Dylan explained all this to me. I never would have known. And I was beginning to think that there might be a perfect recipe for finding love after all.

The normal girl technique was more subtle. You dressed pretty but not overly fancy (you could still ride a bike or play catch in whatever you're wearing), and you might wear a little makeup, but never so the boys could notice it or, God forbid, see you putting it on. You are chatty and fun but not silly or giggly, and you are friendly but not aggressive. You don't travel in big packs and you try to be friends with a boy first. Some boys might be too clueless to realize when a normal girl likes them—that's the bad part—but in the long run, Dylan assured me, you attract better boys with this approach. Most important, the normal girl approach reminded you that boys are not that different from girls. They are people with feelings who are often shy and they just need to be treated with the same consideration you'd give a friend.

"I think I'd rather be a normal girl," I told Dylan.

"Good," Dylan said. "Slow and steady wins the race."

My hand ached after copying all of this down. I couldn't wait to put everything I learned into practice. I only wished I could discuss it all with my best friends.

"Thank you, Dylan," I said. "This is so helpful."

Dylan smiled, looking a little weary after sharing everything she knew.

Just then the phone rang. Would you believe it was Emma, inviting me over? I couldn't get the words out of my mouth fast enough. "Be right over!" I said, and hung up before I made the mistake of asking if Matt was going to be there. I was dying to, but slow and steady wins the race, I reminded myself. I might have to add that to my list of mottoes.

Dylan winked at me. "Go get him, tiger," she said.

"So, I'll let you know how it goes, in case he's there?"

"Who?" Dylan asked.

What? "Dylan!" I cried.

"Kidding!" she said with a laugh.

"Thanks again," I yelled as I ran down the stairs, hopped on my bike, and flew to the Taylors in record time.

CHAPTER 11

Slam Dunk!

$\mathcal{H}$ey," said Emma when I walked in. "You look nice." She circled me and took in my outfit and hair and everything.

My stomach was all butterflies, and I glanced uneasily around the kitchen. "What's up?" I asked. I wasn't going to tell her about the makeover. Not now, anyway.

And then Emma flatly said, "He's not here."

"Who?" I asked, a little taken aback.

Emma made a face. "Lover boy," she said, exasperated.

I blushed. "What?"

"I knew it!" shrieked Emma. "I was just testing you, but now I know for sure!"

"Know what?" I persisted.

Emma leaned in close. "I know you're in love with Matt," she whispered.

"Me? Matt? *What?*" I felt the heat rising in my cheeks.

Emma nodded, a look of satisfaction on her face. "I figured it out yesterday when we saw him at the mall. You got all blushy and nervous and then I saw that kooky notebook on your desk—"

"You did?" I interrupted.

"Ha!" said Emma. "So you are." It was a statement, not a question.

I sighed and looked down at my feet. "Yes. I'm sorry," I mumbled. It felt good to finally admit it, although it felt really weird. I looked at her. "I just can't help it!"

"It's a little awkward," she agreed. "And why Matt? I mean, Sam, maybe. He's cute and girls seem to really like him. But Matt? Smelly sock Matt? Computer geek Matt?"

"Cute, funny, nice Matt," I countered.

"Gross!" Emma exclaimed, playfully slapping me on the shoulder. After a moment she added, "Too bad Callie likes him too."

"Oh!" I said. "I wasn't sure if she liked him or Joe. I thought Sydney might like Matt."

"I can't believe you like my brother," Emma said as she shook her head.

"Well, it's not that surprising. I mean, you and I are good friends, and our moms are good friends. I guess the Taylors and the Beckers are just well-suited to each other!" Emma smiled. "I wonder if he likes you back?" Then she added in a mischievous tone, "Want me to find out?"

"No!" I screamed. "*Please* don't ask him, Emma." I was begging her, but part of me really did want to know.

"Well, at least he'll be at Dylan's party. Even if my mom has to drag him there," said Emma.

"You don't think he wants to go?" I asked, feeling a slight sting.

"No way! He and my mom had a big fight about it. Sam, of course, wants to go, because there'll be all those cute girls there. Jake will go anyplace where there's Mia or cupcakes, and both is even better. Matt is just . . . I don't know. I think he might be kind of shy about girls."

"Really?" I asked, surprised. From what I'd seen, he seemed pretty comfortable with the attention he got from girls. "He doesn't act that way."

Emma thought for a minute. "Hmm . . . I think what I mean is that I don't know if he's mature enough to like girls, you know. The thing he's really into is sports, especially basketball. So you could brush up on your dunking! That's something to put in your notebook."

The notebook! "Look, the notebook was just—"

"Pure Alexis," Emma said, laughing. "Always taking the business approach. Don't worry, I won't tell anyone about it. And I'm sorry for looking at it. I shouldn't have, but I thought it was a math notebook!"

"Yes, you shouldn't have," I replied. But I couldn't be mad at Emma. She was one of my best friends. Besides, I was happy we were talking about Matt!

"Let me see, what other 'data' can I give you?" Emma asked, looking upward and tapping her chin with one finger. "He loves cupcakes. And he's really into computer graphics. Maybe you could call him up and ask him to help on a project for the Cupcake Club? And then pay him in cupcakes?"

"Oooh! Good idea," I lied. As if I'd call him again.

Emma looked at me with a serious expression. "Can I ask you if you want him to be your boyfriend? I can't imagine Matt being anyone's boyfriend, but whatever."

I hesitated. Should I tell Emma my goal? She was my friend, but she was also Matt's sister. She looked at me expectantly. My goal was much easier to explain than any of my other feelings, so I took a deep breath and confessed, "I want to dance with him at Dylan's party."

Emma's eyes widened. "Wow. That's it? It seems like a small thing, but it actually may be impossible to accomplish. I don't think he dances."

I hadn't thought of that! "Well . . . ," I said, not knowing how to respond.

Suddenly the back door opened. "Hello!" hollered Matt.

"Eek!" I squealed. I was totally caught off guard, even though I had been hoping he would show up.

Matt was all sweaty from practice and had on a hideous pair of ripped sweatpants and a T-shirt. His hair was sticking up every which way. But he still looked gorgeous to me.

He seemed surprised to see me. "Oh, hey, Alexis," he said.

My heart leaped. He had said hi first! I couldn't wait to log *that* data in the notebook!

"Got any cupcakes?" he asked.

I laughed nervously. "No. Not yet." Should I ask him a question now? I didn't know what to do or say. Thinking of Sydney, I flipped my hair from one side to the other. "Huh," was all he said before heading for the fridge.

"Where's Mom?" he asked Emma.

"At Jake's practice," Emma replied, then she winked at me. "Hey, Alexis and I were just going out to shoot some hoops. Want to come give us some pointers?"

I stared at her. What was she doing? I couldn't believe what she had just suggested! I looked over at Matt, who was chugging a Gatorade. He turned and looked at us over the rim of the bottle. When he finished, he let out a really loud burp and grinned.

The burp was gross, and I wondered why he felt it was okay to do that in front of me. But then he said, "Sure," and shrugged, and the next thing I knew I was playing H-O-R-S-E in the drive-way with Matt Taylor, man of my dreams! I silently forgave him for burping and quickly got caught up in the game.

I have to say that I am decent at basketball. Not sure why, but maybe because it's kind of like danc-ing to me. I don't know. Anyway, we were having a pretty good time. I think Matt was even impressed by my skills. This was definitely the normal girl approach, and it seemed to be working.

After about fifteen minutes, Joe Fraser showed up, and he joined the game too. I was so happy! Emma and I challenged the boys to a two-on-two, but they insisted we split the teams, so Matt and I played Joe and Emma. It was awesome. We were winning, 8 to 2, when suddenly somebody called out, "Yoo-hoo!"

Sydney and Callie!

Emma and I looked at each other and frowned. I couldn't tell if Matt and Joe were happy or annoyed. But the girls were definitely happy. They were super dressed up for a Sunday morning, in skin-tight jeans and tight sweaters with tiny down vests, and boots with high heels. Their hair was super-fluffy and they had on tons of makeup and perfume and dangly earrings. I wondered when Sydney had planned this little outing.

"Can we play?" asked Sydney in her high, flirty voice. Callie at least had the grace to look nervous.

Matt shrugged. "Okay." He didn't sound excited, but he didn't sound mad, either. I think he was just being polite. Emma, on the other hand, was really mad. Her face was set like stone.

"I think we need to play H-O-R-S-E again," said Matt.

"What's that?" Callie said, giggling.

Matt explained the game, and he went first, tossing the ball in high over his left shoulder, facing away from the basket. It was an impressive shot.

Sydney clapped and whistled, and Matt grinned. Why hadn't I thought to praise him like that? Then she stepped up to take the shot and threw it so badly that it just flew over her shoulder, landing nowhere near the basket.

"Whoops!" she said with a laugh, covering her mouth with a hand that showed off fresh scarlet nail polish. Sydney clearly didn't care that she had missed. In fact, she probably missed on purpose.

Callie took the ball. She bounced it once or twice, then flipped it over her shoulder, but her sweater was so tight it made her lose control as the ball left her hand; it fell weakly to the ground and rolled away. "Oh dear! I stink!" Callie said, but it was clear she didn't really care how badly she played either.

Now it was my turn. If ever I had wanted something in my life, this was it. I focused like a laser beam and took a deep breath, closing my eyes. Then I bent my knees like Matt had and lifted the ball in a gentle arc over my shoulder. *Slow and steady wins the race,* I told myself. I didn't dare to look, but when I heard the ball thump the backboard and

Matt yelling, my eyes flew open. Matt had both fists straight in the air. "Yes!" he cried. "You made it!" He stuck out his hand for a high five and I slapped it, laughing in giddy relief.

I stole a quick glance at Callie and Sydney and they were both standing there with their mouths open. Sydney started chewing on the end of a piece of her fluffy hair, probably wondering what she should do next. I had a new equation for my workbook:

Sports skills + comfortable clothes = boys impressed by YOU!

A few minutes later Mrs. Taylor pulled up to drop off Jake and pick up Matt and Joe to go to their friend's house for a school project. I didn't really get the chance to say good-bye to Matt, but it was all good. I was still on a high from my totally awesome shot.

"Let's hit it," Sydney said to Callie as soon as the boys left. Sydney didn't bother to say good-bye to Emma and me, but Callie turned to us with an awkward expression. "Well, thanks . . . ," she said.

"See ya," Emma muttered without bothering to look in their direction. We went inside, and Jake immediately went for the couch in the TV room. Emma started to make him a snack in the kitchen.

"Wow," I said.

"I can't believe you made that basket!" said Emma, laughing.

"Me neither!" I howled. "Talk about luck!"

"It was skill," said Emma. "And Matt was impressed."

"You think?" I asked, but I knew he was. My chest was bursting with pride and happiness.

As we headed to the TV room with drinks and Jake's snack, Emma said, "We still have to figure out Dylan's dessert. Let's get the others over here and bake."

"Yay! Cupcakes!" Jake yelled.

"Good idea," I agreed, thinking of the extra cupcakes we could leave behind for Matt!

CHAPTER 12

Confession

Of course, after that wonderful Sunday morning, I didn't see Matt for an entire week. I wore each of the outfits that Dylan had planned for me, and I took great care with my hair (down) and makeup, but no luck. My friends all noticed the change though, and Mia and Katie pestered me about my new look. I was happy that Emma did not let on about my crush, but it wasn't long before they figured it out.

It happened while we were sitting at lunch one day, when Sydney and Callie came over to our table.

"Hey, Emma," said Sydney. We all looked up in shock. Sydney usually just ignores us and rarely calls us by name.

"Oh, hey," Emma replied like she didn't care.

"We have a question. Someone said Matt is going to Dylan Becker's sweet sixteen on the twentieth. Is that true?" She was asking about my sister's party and she didn't even look at me! My blood began to boil.

Emma looked at me and raised her eyebrows. She turned to Sydney. "Yes. Our whole family is going."

"We're all going, actually," said Mia in a cold, snooty voice I'd never heard her use before.

I seemed to have lost my ability to speak.

Sydney and Callie exchanged a look. "Okay, thanks," said Sydney, before she and Callie walked away, their heads bent close as they whispered.

"What was that all about?" I burst out. "Wouldn't you think they would ask me? It's *my* sister they're talking about! And why do they want to know, anyway? It's not like they're invited!"

"They have some nerve," said Katie, shaking her head.

"I am so sick of those two. They just can't leave Matt alone. Someone keeps calling and hanging up, and I swear it's them!" Emma complained.

My stomach flip-flopped. They were calling Matt? That was pretty major!

"Has he actually *spoken* to them on the phone?" I asked, probably with a little too much feeling, because Mia and Katie turned to me with raised eyebrows.

Emma shrugged. "I'm not sure," she answered.

I could feel Mia still watching me. Then she asked with a shy smile, "Alexis, is there something you want to tell us?"

I was so bothered by Sydney that I simply admitted, "Yes, I have a crush on Matt." Then I added, "I'm sure you all already know."

"I didn't tell them!" Emma cried out defensively, even though I didn't look at her.

Katie immediately jumped on Emma. "Wait, you knew?" she asked.

Uh-oh. This had the makings of a cupcake war. I had to stop it before it went too far. "I'm sorry, guys," I told Katie and Mia. "I was going to tell you guys, but there just never seemed to be a right time."

"Well, there was clearly a right time to tell Emma, it seems!" Mia said, sounding a little offended, but I don't think she was actually mad.

"Oh, no, I guessed, actually," Emma said, "and made Alexis fess up. Then she swore me to secrecy. It is just too weird. I can't imagine anyone liking my brother, but now it seems he's getting all this attention from girls."

"Humph!" I said, and crossed my arms.

"So what are you doing about this crush?" Mia asked me.

"I've been doing some research," I said without thinking, and my friends all burst out laughing.

"Research!" Mia yelled. "Alexis, that is just so typical of you!"

"Wait, is that why you've had this sudden make-over and everything?" Katie asked.

I nodded shyly and muttered, "A lot of good it's doing. I've barely even seen him since."

"But it worked when you did see him!" said Emma.

"You think?" I asked, hoping that all my work wasn't going to waste.

Emma nodded. "Hello? He came out and played basketball with us!"

"You don't think he was just . . . bored or trying to be nice?" I pressed.

Emma shook her head. "Uh-uh. He would never be nice for no reason."

"Actually, I think he's really nice. Like when he helped you—"

"All right, all right! We know *you* think he's

nice," interrupted Emma. "I guess he is a little bit. I'm just not sure he's worth the time and effort, that's all."

"Yes, well, if he was a client, I think I would have stopped my aggressive marketing efforts by now," I said, and everyone laughed again.

"So when you say you have a crush on him, what does that mean?" asked Katie.

"Oh, I think he's cute. I want him to like me back. And . . ." I looked over at Emma, and she finished what I was too embarrassed to say.

"She wants to dance with him at Dylan's sweet sixteen."

I bit my lip nervously, unsure how my friends would react. But I didn't have to worry.

Mia clapped excitedly. "Ooh! Once he sees you dance he will fall head over heels in love with you!"

Katie grinned. "Are you going to ask *him*?"

"I haven't quite worked that part out yet," I admitted.

"Between the dancing and the cupcakes, I know he'll be wowed," said Katie loyally.

"Anything we can do to help?" asked Mia.

As much as I wanted to keep talking about Matt, I suddenly remembered there was something more important that we needed to do. "Yes! Let's figure out those cupcakes!" At least that was something that I could control. "Dylan has been on a rampage, so we need to sort it out before she goes nuts. The only thing is, she's also been really nice to me lately, with the makeover and stuff. I think she's just stressed. Let's give her the works!"

"The works?" Katie asked.

"I've been thinking," I said. "Let's forget about the budget for now. Instead, we should wrap up all of our great ideas into one slam dunk of a cupcake."

Emma smiled. "So what is it?"

"The s'mores disco gift cupcake. Chocolate cupcake filled with marshmallow, topped with chocolate frosting with graham cracker and gold flake crumble, and tied with a gold bow. She'll love it. And it will cheer her up."

The girls all agreed, so we made plans to start working on the cupcakes soon.

Dylan had, in fact, been even crankier than ever this week. As the RSVPs for her party rolled in, she became compulsive about checking voice mail and the list. I wondered if there was someone special she was waiting to hear from. Dylan is class president and assistant cheer captain, so I knew she wasn't exactly lacking for friends or popularity. But as I watched her flip through the RSVP notebook one afternoon, I kind of felt sorry for her.

"What's up?" I asked.

"Nothing," she replied. *Flip, flip, flip.*

I tried again. "Are you waiting to hear from someone?" I asked.

Dylan stopped flipping and sighed heavily. "*Don't* ever fall in love, Alexis."

"Too late, Dyl, I'm a goner," I said. "Who are you in love with?"

"Never mind," she said. "Nothing will come of it. He hasn't even RSVP'd."

"Sounds like a jerk," I said. The invitations had been out for days. Whoever she was talking about should have already received it.

But Dylan had bristled. "No, no, no, he's not a jerk," she replied defensively. "He's just very busy! I'm sure he'll . . . he'll let me know soon."

"Okay!" I said brightly, not wanting to upset her. But inside I thought, *Why do boys cause such heartache?*

That night, when my mother came in to say good night, I told her, "Mom, I think I know why Dylan's been such a jerk lately." I'd been puzzling over it all evening, and I was pretty sure I was right.

"Why? I'd love to know!"

"I think she's in love with someone and he might not love her back."

"Hmm . . . that *would* explain a lot."

"I think she wants everything to be perfect at the party so he'll fall in love with her."

"Oh! Is he coming?"

"Well, that's the other thing. He hasn't RSVP'd."

"Poor Dylly."

I nodded and sighed. At least the love of my life was coming. Granted his mother had RSVP'd for him, but it was a start!

"Well, I'll see if I can discuss it with her," Mom said before pulling the covers up tight under my chin. "I love you, sweetheart. Thanks for the tip."

"Of course, Mom. Love you, too."

CHAPTER 13
not
BF∧F 😟

The day of Dylan's party was gorgeous: The sky was blue, the sun was shining, and birds were literally singing in the trees. It promised to be a beautiful night. But first there was lots of baking to be done!

The Cupcake Club met at Mia's that morning, which was a good thing, even though I was bummed not to have a chance to see Matt. It was better, because I could focus on making our cupcakes.

We ended up going with my idea of combining all three original cupcake ideas. Dylan had surprised us when she said she "loved" this idea. But these were going to take a lot longer to decorate, so we had to be really organized.

We had an assembly line going once the cupcakes were baked and cooled. I lifted them off the cooling rack in their gold foil papers and filled them with liquid marshmallow using a baker's syringe. Then Katie would frost the cupcakes with dark chocolate frosting, and Emma would add the crumbled graham crackers and gold sprinkles. Finally Mia would tie the base of each one with a big gold ribbon, and set it back on the cooling racks to pack later.

Even though I wasn't anywhere near Matt, I was glad to have him on my mind as Katie and Mia kept asking me questions.

"What position does he play on the basketball team?" Mia asked.

"Oh, point guard, I think," I said.

"Center," corrected Emma.

"Right. I always get those mixed up."

"Have you been to any of his games yet?" asked Katie.

"No, but I think I'm going to go this week. Anyone want to go with me?"

"I always go," said Emma, "if I can. We have a rule in our family that if you can possibly make it to a sibling's game, you have to go, to show support."

"Let me know if he ever needs any extra support!" I said, laughing. "I can always sub for you if you can't make it!"

Emma's response was to playfully stick her tongue out at me. I stuck mine right back at her.

"So what are his favorite cupcakes we've made so far?" Mia asked.

I didn't know the answers to any of their questions, but I wanted them to think I knew something about Matt.

"Oh, I think the . . ." I looked around.

"Bacon," said Emma. "He liked the caramel cupcakes with the bacon caramel frosting. He had me make them for his team dinner."

"Runs in the family!" Mia laughed. The recipe had been Emma's idea.

"He also liked the mini vanillas we made for Mona," I added.

Emma shook her head. "That boy would eat anything if you frosted it."

The vanilla minis were *my* recipe! "Well, he certainly wolfed them down," I retorted.

"Alexis, you don't live with him like I do," Emma insisted. "He even eats burnt cupcakes, as long as they're loaded with frosting."

"Wait a second," I protested, suddenly getting

mad. "Are you comparing my vanilla minis to burnt cupcakes?" I couldn't believe Emma was so rude! She was supposed to be on *my* side.

"Okay, you two," Katie said as she exchanged a look with Mia.

"I just don't know who made you the Matt expert all of a sudden," said Emma. "You barely know him!"

"That's not true!" I said. But it kind of was.

"The only times you ever interact with him, I'm there! So how could you suddenly have this great romance blooming?"

Now I was really mad. "There's no 'great romance blooming,' Emma. I just think he's really cute. And the time when I decided I liked him, you *weren't* there!"

"Well, it's annoying! I'm sick of hearing you talk about him like you own him! You're no better than Sydney Whitman!"

"It's Callie who likes him." I spat the words out furiously.

"Well, it's Sydney who's doing all the work!" said Emma. "Just like me for you!"

"What?"

"Stop, you guys!" cried Katie. "Come on!"

Emma and I glared at each other.

118

"Speaking of work, we have a whole lot of cupcakes to bake," said Mia, sounding like a parent. "And we need to get them all done today. Business first, Alexis. That's your motto."

"So let's just focus on what we need to do, okay?" Katie added.

I nodded without looking at Emma. I decided I would not speak to her. In fact, I would not speak at all.

Emma muttered something, but I didn't care to ask what she said. I was all business now. For the next few hours, I worked quickly to fill two hundred cupcakes, and by noon we were done. I only talked when Mia and Katie spoke to me. No one was happy that things were tense, but it wasn't *my* fault!

Mom came to pick up the cupcakes and take them to the restaurant. Mia, Katie, and Emma had plans to dress together for the party, and I wasn't happy about that. I didn't want them to all be having fun without me (or worse, talking about me), but I couldn't ditch my family, and it would just be too hectic to have my friends get ready at my house, what with Dylan's chaos going on.

Dylan's crush still had not RSVP'd, which made him uncrushworthy in my book. But I think she was still hoping. Every time the phone rang that afternoon, she dashed to check the caller ID (not that she'd answer the phone, because that would seem desperate).

Meredith and Skylar came over to get ready with Dylan, almost like bridesmaids before a wedding. They were all in black and gold, of course, and when they were ready, they offered to help me with my hair and makeup. Of course I said yes!

Meredith was working on my hair with rollers. "Is there anyone special coming tonight that you're looking forward to seeing?" she asked.

I narrowed my eyes at Dylan. "Did you tell her?" I snapped.

"No, Alexis," Dylan calmly replied. "I didn't say anything to anyone."

"Chill, Alexis, she didn't," Meredith said, a little taken aback. "I was just asking to make conversation, like they do at the hairdresser."

I felt bad. "Oh, sorry. Actually, there is one guy I like. He's . . . he's my friend's older brother. But she's mad at me right now for liking him."

"That's ridiculous! She doesn't own him!" said Meredith.

"I know!" I felt myself getting riled up all over again.

"And it's not like she could marry him, anyway!" she added, laughing.

"You're so right!"

"That happened with me at day camp one summer," Skylar joined in. "I lost a friend that way. I totally regret it."

"What do you mean?" I asked.

"Well, I was about your age, and there was this really cute junior counselor named Tom. And his sister Madison was my best friend at camp. But I became so obsessed with Tom that every time I called Madison, every time I went to their house, it was like it was really to catch a glimpse of Tom. Madison ended up feeling like I was using her just to get to Tom."

"Were you?"

"No! I really liked Madison! It was just inconvenient that the guy I liked happened to be her brother!"

"Well, it was also probably convenient, too," I said knowingly.

Skylar nodded. "Sure, because I got the insider's perspective, and I got to see him casually, without having to go on a date or anything. I could see him in his normal environment."

"But you lost a friend," said Meredith.

"Yes, a good friend," Skylar replied. "And I was so over him by the end of the summer."

"How did you get over him?" I asked.

"We finally went on a date, and I realized we had nothing to talk about when Madison wasn't there."

Just then the phone rang. I was holding the cordless in my lap, and I flipped it over to see what the caller ID said.

"Hanson?" I said aloud.

Dylan screamed, "It's him! Get it! No wait, don't!" But it was too late.

"Hello?" I said.

A deep voice kind of stammered, "Uh . . . hi . . . is Dylan there, please?"

I looked at Dylan and she was shaking her head no.

"Um, no, I'm sorry, she's out right now," I lied. "May I take a message?"

"Yes. This is Noah Hanson. I'm so embarrassed. Dylan invited me to her party, and the invitation got mixed up with my mother's bills, and I only just opened it. I know it's too late to say yes, so I was just calling to apologize. Will you tell her, please?"

I froze for a second.

"Hello?" he said again.

"No! Come! It's not too late! It's . . . a buffet. One more person won't make a difference. Don't worry. Just come! I'm sure she'd be happy to see you." I said, crossing my fingers. *Please say yes, please say yes.* I hoped for Dylan's sake.

He paused. "Well, if you think it's okay . . . Um, who is this?"

"I'm Alexis, her sister, and my mom is here, and she's nodding, so it's totally fine for you to come," I lied again, holding my crossed fingers up in the air. I looked over at Dylan. Her face was hidden in her hands as she waited for the final verdict.

"Oh, okay, that's really nice," Noah said, sounding very relieved. "Thanks! So, I'll be there at seven, right?"

"Yup, seven it is. See you there!" I sang out and uncrossed my fingers to switch to a thumbs-up sign before hanging up.

"Yessss!" Dylan screamed as soon as I put the phone back on its base. "Oh, Alexis, you are the best! Thank you, thank you so much!" She jumped up and grabbed me in a big hug.

She and Meredith and Skylar started yelling and dancing around together in a circle. "Yay! Noah's coming!"

At that moment Mom poked her head in to see what the noise was all about. "He's coming," I whispered. She didn't need to ask who.

"Phew," she said, and with a wink, she closed the door.

This was going to be a great night.

CHAPTER 14

Nothing > Friends!

$\mathcal{G}$irls, you look spectacular!" my father said proudly as he wrapped his arms around Dylan and me for the photographer.

"Gorgeous," my mother agreed.

"You two look pretty great, yourselves," I said. And they did.

We had arrived early, along with Meredith and Skylar, to make sure everything was set up just right. I checked the cupcakes first, of course, but the restaurant had arranged them beautifully on three tiers of a gold cake stand. They looked really pretty and I knew they'd taste even better!

Dylan looked really happy about the cupcakes and gave me a hug as we stood in front of the display. "Thank you," she whispered. She looked really beautiful in her gown, and I even started to tear up a little. I think I was just relieved that we were done with all those weeks of arguing, the cupcakes were done, and this day was finally here!

I watched as Dylan glanced nervously at the front doors. I knew how she felt. I kept waiting to see handsome Matt walk through the door myself (never mind that he'd be with Emma!) and had gone to the ladies' room twice to check my appearance in the mirror.

I had worn my hair down and in loopy curls (thanks to Meredith). I had on a little bit of Mom-approved makeup and a tiny bit of vanilla spice perfume (thanks to Dylan). I was wearing the fuzzy pink dress (thanks to Mia) with a gold chain belt of my mother's and some gold sandals of Dylan's. I had a chunky ice-cube necklace from Mia, and it looked fantastic. I had to admit, I was looking pretty good.

The band was warming up, and my father asked them to play a little bit of "The Way You Look Tonight," so we could practice our dance. They played the whole thing and when we finished our dance, the whole band applauded!

Just before seven, people started to arrive. That's when I got really, really nervous. Luckily,

Mia and Katie arrived together right at the start. Emma had gone home after getting ready, so she could come with her family. I wasn't sure what I would say to her when she came. Still, I watched the door eagerly for the arrival of the Taylors— and for Noah!

Mia and Katie were getting a soda by the bar and I was saying hi to Dylan's godmother when Sydney and Callie walked in! And would you believe Callie was wearing that black *Dancing with the Stars*-type dress from Icon!

I rushed over to Dylan. "Look who's here!" I said angrily, grabbing her arm.

She looked at the door, just as a gorgeous, tall, blond guy walked in.

"Noah!" she screamed.

"Noah? No, no, not him!" I said. "He's cute though! No, Sydney and Callie are here! There they are!" I pointed across the room to where they were standing.

"Did you invite them?" Dylan asked as she hurried to the door to meet Noah. She didn't seem concerned at all that the devilish duo had crashed her party!

"Of course not!" I said, trying to keep up with her.

"Callie is Jenna Wilson's little sister, right? Jenna's here," said Dylan. Of course! Callie's older sister was on cheerleading with Dylan. So of course she'd be invited, but that didn't explain Callie and Sydney.

"Why don't you go find out why they're here?" Dylan said just as we got to the door. "I'm going to say hi to Noah."

I watched as Noah kissed Dylan on the cheek, and then Dylan took his hand, guiding him toward the drinks. I was happy for Dylan that Noah showed up, but superannoyed that she wasn't mad that Sydney and Callie had shown up at her party uninvited! (And after the hard time she'd given me about inviting my friends!)

I stared at Sydney and Callie for a minute, trying to figure out what I wanted to do. Just then Callie pulled Sydney with her across the room, toward an older girl who I now recognized as Callie's sister. Jenna had been talking with her friends, and turned around when Callie tapped her on the shoulder. Jenna seemed genuinely shocked to see Callie and Sydney and looked really annoyed.

Mia and Katie came over. "Did you invite them?" Mia asked, nodding her head toward Sydney and Callie.

"As if!" I said.

"Then why are they here?" Katie asked.

"I . . . ," I started to say, but then something—or rather, some*one*—caught my eye. It was Emma, with the rest of the Taylors. I wanted to run across the room to greet them, but then I remembered my fight with Emma, and I held back.

I checked my dress and my hair, patting everything nervously as the Taylors walked toward me. Jake looked really cute in a little jacket and tie, and Matt and even Sam looked, frankly, gorgeous in their suits.

"Hi, Alexis, darling! Don't you look beautiful!" Mrs. Taylor said, greeting me with a kiss. Mr. Taylor did the same as Mrs. Taylor looked around the room. "Now, where's your mom? Wow, it looks wonderful in here! What a lot of planning you've all done! Oh, there she is. I'll go say hello. Come on, sweetie." And Emma's parents took off, leaving their kids standing with me.

Jake went up to Mia and tugged on her dress to say hi, and they and Katie began chatting about law enforcement, Jake's favorite subject.

Sam said, "Great party. Oh, wow, there's Dylan!" and he walked over to her.

Then it was just me, Matt, and Emma. It felt

really awkward. I hadn't made eye contact with Emma yet.

"Hey, would you guys like a soda?" I finally said, looking somewhere between the two of them.

"Sure," Matt answered. "Why don't I get something for you two?"

Emma and I looked at each other, and suddenly we both burst out laughing. Hard! We couldn't stay mad at each other, especially not on such a big night.

Emma put her arm through mine. "Sure," she told Matt. "I'll have a Sprite."

"Me too, thanks," I said, giving him my best smile.

Matt grinned, and as he walked away I pretended to swoon. "He is too cute!" I whispered. "Sorry!"

"It's okay," said Emma. "I'm sorry I was so mean earlier. I guess it was just a little hard to take."

"I know I've been kind of annoying about it," I said, thinking about the story Skylar told earlier. "Anyway, I would never sacrifice our friendship for love. If it came down to Matt being my boyfriend or you being my friend, I'd pick you. I swear."

Emma looked like she didn't believe me, but she hugged me and said, "Thanks, but I don't think you need to make a choice. I love my brother too, you know." She swatted my arm playfully, then gasped.

I looked over to see what she was looking at and rolled my eyes. I had, for five minutes, forgotten about Sydney and Callie, but there they were, still standing around. "Yeah, can you believe they had the nerve to show up?"

"Unbelievable!" Emma said in a disgusted tone. When Katie and Mia came back (without Jake, who was now with his mother), we started trying to figure out what we should do. We decided that Emma would say something to Sydney, since Sydney had approached her about the party in the first place. I wondered if we should kick them out, but Mia thought that wouldn't be very ladylike and suggested we tell the manager that there were crashers.

Emma took a deep breath before crossing the dance floor toward Sydney and Callie, who had just spotted Matt. I watched in horror as they surrounded him, and Sydney snaked her arm through his. It made me wonder about Emma's comment about Sydney doing all the work for Callie. Maybe Sydney secretly liked Matt herself.

When Emma joined them, she began talking, and they were all listening to what she was saying. Then Sydney began gesturing and telling some sort of story. Matt watched the whole thing in silence, I was glad to see, and when the bartender handed him the sodas, he took them in his hands and took a few steps away from the group.

Emma must have made Sydney and Callie feel bad enough to leave, because Callie suddenly grabbed Sydney's arm and was pulling her toward the door. I hoped they would leave!

When Emma and Matt came back with the drinks, Emma looked really mad, but Matt was laughing.

"I hate those two. They are so evil!" Emma exclaimed. "They said Callie's sister, Jenna, had 'lost' her precious cell phone, so they had to deliver it to her. They didn't want to look out of place, so they dressed up."

I looked at Sydney and Callie, slowly making their way to the door. "I wonder how it got 'lost' in the first place if it was so precious?"

"Exactly! So I told them to go," said Emma.

Matt was still laughing. "The drama with all you girls!" he said. "I can't believe it. It's so dumb!"

"Believe it, mister," said Emma as she took our drinks from him.

"Thank you," I said to Matt. But as I took a sip, I saw my mother talking to Sydney and Callie at the door. She seemed to be guiding them toward the refreshments instead of the door! What was she doing?

Now Sydney and Callie headed toward us. That made me madder than ever, and when I am mad, I think the adrenaline makes me do things I would normally be too afraid to do! I looked over at Matt, and he was looking at them, then at Emma, then at me. And right then he and I both said at the same time, "Wanna dance?"

I couldn't believe it! I know where my courage came from (the adrenaline from being mad!), but I will never know what made Matt ask me to dance. I don't know if Emma said something to him before the party, or his mom, or if he decided it himself, but whatever it was, the timing was great.

Matt and I laughed and hit the dance floor just as Sydney and Callie arrived where we'd been standing. Emma winked at me and went off with Mia and Katie to get some hors d'oeuvres.

The truth is, Matt and I didn't have anything to say to each other. We smiled a lot, and since I am a good dancer, I think I impressed him. He is an okay dancer, but for someone so athletic, he's not that great. I don't want to say I fell a little out of love with him right then, but between Emma's and my friendship being on the line, us having nothing to say to each other, and him being only a so-so dancer, my crush kind of lost a little fizzle that night. And I was okay with that. I was proud to have set a goal, and to have reached it!

As Matt and I danced, I thought about all of my equations and my research. Oh, I was superhappy the whole time I was with Matt, but I decided that when it comes to love, there is no perfect recipe. There are so many ingredients, and things just have to happen naturally. If you need to force them or manipulate them, then they just aren't meant to be.

There was a lot of crushing going on that night at Dylan's party: I liked Matt, Callie liked Matt, maybe even Sydney liked Matt, Dylan liked Noah, Sam liked Dylan . . . and I'm sure there were a lot more equations that may not have a solution. All I know is this:

$$Nothing > friends$$

I repeat: Nothing is greater than friends!

CHAPTER 15

Later that Night . . .

Dylan's friends freaked out over the cupcakes. People came up to her all night to rave about them, and in the end, Dylan declared that the s'mores disco gift cupcakes made the party. That and Noah coming. They had a plan to go to the movies the very next night, which just goes to show you that if something is meant to happen, it just does.

For me, what made the party were the dance with Matt, the look on Callie's and Sydney's faces when he and I danced, making up with Emma, Dylan loving the cupcakes, and my big moment on the dance floor with Dad. Everyone gathered around and cheered. We were so good! We would have won if it was a contest! At the end he gave me a big hug and said, "Alexis, you are wonderful.

Just the way you are!" I looked over and saw Matt smiling at us, and I smiled back.

When we got home that night (along with Meredith and Skylar, who were sleeping over), I opened my locked drawer and took out the Matt notebook. It had been fun doing the research online and reading all the studies and their results, but it had been hard to quantify the results in a real-life setting. I needed data that was more concrete. And real feedback. Like tonight. I had reached my goal, and I could cross it off in my planner. Matt and I had danced together.

I read a quote somewhere that said, "The essence of mathematics is not to make simple things complicated, but to make complicated things simple." Someone named Gudder said it. I think he or she was right. The whole math thing complicated a simple crush. But on the bright side, I got a great makeover, some good love advice, and a dance with a cute boy. It was all good.

I wasn't sure what would happen next with Matt, if anything, or if I even wanted anything to. I needed a new goal, whether it was love-related or not, because when it comes down to it, I am all about setting and reaching my goals. Failing to plan is planning to fail. That's one of my mottoes.

So maybe it was time to focus on business again, instead of love. One thing is for sure: If I'd spent as much time on the Cupcake Club this month as I did on Matt, my friends and I would all be a lot richer!

I ripped the pages out of the Matt notebook. Then I dumped them into the shredder under my desk. It was time for a new goal. I picked up my planner again and on a new goal page I wrote:

SELL MORE CUPCAKES!

I sent an e-mail to the Cupcake Club:

> Great work! Thanks for putting up with Dylan. And me. Now on to the next assignment!
> xoxo,
> Alexis

Then I grabbed some SweeTarts and went to see if anyone wanted to watch *Dancing with the Stars* with me.

Want another sweet cupcake?
Here's a sneak peek
of the fifth book in the

CUPCAKE  DIARIES

series:

Katie,
batter up!

My Cupcake Obsession

My name is Katie Brown, and I am crazy about cupcakes. I'm not kidding. I think about cupcakes every day. I even dream about them when I sleep. The other night I was dreaming that I was eating a giant cupcake, and when I woke up I was chewing on my pillow!

Okay, now I am kidding. But I do dream about cupcakes, I swear. There must be a name for this condition. Cupcake-itis? That's got to be it. I am stricken with cupcake-itis, and there isn't any cure.

My three best friends and I formed the Cupcake Club, and we bake cupcakes for parties and events and things and sell them. We're all different in our own way. Mia has dark brown hair and loves fashion. Emma has blond hair and blue eyes, and lots of brothers. Alexis has curly red hair and loves math. (Can you believe it? But she really does!)

I have light brown hair, and I mostly wear jeans and T-shirts. I'm an only child. And I hate math. But I have one big thing in common with all my friends: We love cupcakes.

That's why we were in my kitchen on a Tuesday afternoon, baking cupcakes on a beautiful spring day. We were having an official meeting to discuss our next big job: baking a cupcake cake for my Grandma Carole's seventy-fifth birthday bash. But while we were thinking about that, we were also trying to perfect a new chocolate-coconut-almond cupcake, specially created for my friend Mia's step-dad, Eddie, based on his favorite candy bar.

We had tried two different combinations already: a chocolate cupcake with coconut frosting and almonds on top, and a coconut cupcake with chocolate-almond frosting, but none of them matched the taste of the candy bar enough. Now we were working on a third batch: a chocolate-almond cupcake with coconut frosting and lots of shredded coconut on top.

I carefully poured a teaspoon of almond extract into the batter. "Mmm . . . smells almond-y," I said.

"I hope this batch is the one," said Mia. "Eddie

finally started taking down that gross flowery wall-paper in my bedroom, and I have to find some way to thank him. I would have paid someone a million dollars to do that!"

"You realize you could buy a whole new house for a million dollars, right?" Alexis asked. "Probably two or three."

"You know what I mean," Mia replied. "Besides, you know how ugly that wallpaper is. It looks like something you'd find in an old lady's room."

"Hey, my Grandma Carole's an old lady, and she doesn't have ugly wallpaper in her house," I protested.

Emma picked up the ice-cream scoop and started scooping up the batter and putting it into the cup-cake pans.

"We need to find out more about your grandma," Emma said. "That way we can figure out what kind of cupcakes to make for the party."

"Right!" Alexis agreed. She flipped open her notebook and took out the pen tucked behind her ear. Sometimes I think Alexis must have a secret stash of notebooks in her house somewhere. I've never seen her without one.

"First things first," Alexis said. "How many people are coming to the party?"

I wrinkled my nose, thinking. "Not sure," I said. Then I yelled as loud as I could. "Mom! How many people are coming to Grandma Carole's party?"

My mom appeared in the kitchen doorway. "Katie, you know how I feel about yelling," she said.

"Sorry, Mom," I said in my best apology voice.

"The answer is about thirty people," Mom said. "So I think if the cupcake cake has three dozen cupcakes, that would be fine."

"What exactly is a cupcake cake, anyway?" Mia asked. "Do you mean like one of those giant cupcakes that you bake with a special pan?"

"I was thinking more like a bunch of cupcakes arranged in tiers to look like a cake," Mom replied.

Mia nodded to Alexis. "May I?"

"Sure," Alexis replied, handing her the pen and notebook. Mia began to sketch. She's a great artist and wants to be a fashion designer some day.

"Like this?" Mia asked, showing mom the drawing. I looked over Mia's shoulder and saw the plan: three round tiers, one on top of the other, with cupcakes on each one.

"Exactly!" Mom said, smiling and showing off a mouth full of perfect white teeth. (She is a dentist, after all.)

Alexis took back her notebook. "Excellent,"

she said, jotting something down. "Now we just need to decide what flavor to make and how to decorate it."

"What do you think, Mom?" I asked.

"I think I'll let you girls come up with something," Mom replied. "You always come up with such wonderful ideas, and I know Grandma Carole will love whatever you do."

"All done!" Emma announced, putting down the ice-cream scoop.

"Mom, oven, please?" I asked.

"Sure thing," Mom said, slipping on an oven mitt. She put the chocolate-almond cupcakes into the preheated oven, and I set the cupcake-shaped timer on the counter for twenty minutes.

Mom left the kitchen, and the four of us sat down at the kitchen table to work out the details.

"So what kind of flavors does your grandmother like?" Alexis asked.

I shrugged. "I don't know. She likes all kinds of things. Blueberry pie in the summer, and chocolate cake, and maple-walnut ice cream . . ."

"So we can make blueberry-chocolate-maple cupcakes with walnuts on top!" Mia joked, and everyone laughed.

"Hey, we thought bacon flavor was weird and that

worked out well!" said Emma. It was true. Bacon flavor was a really big seller for us.

"You know, we don't know anything about your grandma," Emma said. "Maybe if you tell us something about her we can get some ideas."

"Sure," I said. "Hold on a minute."

I went into the den, where Mom and I keep all of our books and picked up a photo album. We have lots of them, and there were pictures of Grandma Carole in almost all of them. I turned to a photo of my mom and me with Grandma Carole and Grandpa Chuck at Christmas. Grandma Carole looked nice in a red sweater and the beaded necklace I made her as a present at camp. Her hair used to be brown like mine, but now it's white.

"That's her," I said. "And that's my Grandpa Chuck. They got married like forever ago, and they have three kids, my mom and my Uncle Mike and my Uncle Jimmy. She used to be a librarian."

"Just like my mom!" Emma said, smiling.

I flipped the pages in the photo album and found a picture of Grandma Carole in her white tennis outfit, holding her racket.

"Mostly she loves sports and stuff," I said. "She runs like, every day, and she won track medals in high school. She goes swimming, and plays tennis, and skis in the winter, and she likes golf even though she says there's not enough running."

"Do sports have a flavor?" Mia mused.

"Um, sports-drink-flavored cupcakes?" Alexis offered.

"Or sweat-flavored cupcakes," I said, then burst out giggling.

"Katie, that is so gross!" Emma squealed.

"But I guess she does like sports most of all," I said. "She's always trying to get me to do stuff with her. Because I am *soooo* good at sports."

I said that really sarcastically because the exact opposite is true. Now it was Emma's turn to giggle.

"Yeah, I've seen you in gym," she said.

"It's even worse than you know," I confessed. "When she tried to teach me to ski, I wiped out on the bunny hill—you know, the one for little kids? I even sprained my ankle."

"Oh, that's terrible!" Emma cried.

"And when I played tennis on a team with Grandpa, I accidentally whacked him in the head with my racket."

Mia put a hand to her mouth to try to stop laughing. "Oh, Katie, that would be funny if it weren't so terrible!" she said.

I nodded. "He needed four stitches."

"So I guess you don't take after your grandmother," Alexis said.

"Well, not the sports thing," I admitted. "But everyone says I look exactly like she did when she was younger. And she's a good baker, too. She used to own her own cake-baking business."

Alexis stood up. "You're kidding! Why didn't you tell us?"

"I just did," I said.

"But she's a professional," Alexis said. "It's not going to be easy to impress her."

"Yes, the pressure is on," Mia agreed.

I hadn't thought of that before. "Well, we'll just have to make a superawesome cupcake cake then."

Alexis sat back down. "Okay, people, let's start jotting down some ideas."

We tried for the next few minutes, but nobody could think of anything. Then Emma looked at her watch.

"You know, I need to get home," she said. "It's my turn to make dinner tonight."

"We need some time to come up with ideas anyway," Alexis said. "Let's schedule another meeting."

"Let's do it tomorrow," I suggested. But Alexis and Mia had whipped out their smartphones and

Emma took a little notebook with flowers on it—and they were all frowning.

"Alexis and I have soccer practice tomorrow and Thursday, and a game on Friday," Mia reported.

"I have concert band practice on Wednesdays and Fridays," Emma said. Emma plays the flute and she's really good at that.

"Sorry, Katie. You know spring is a busy time of year," Alexis said.

"Yeah, sure," I said, but really, I didn't. I don't really do anything besides the Cupcake Club, and it's not just because I have cupcake-itis. I'm no good at sports, and I'm not so great at music, either. When we learned how to play recorder in fourth grade I ended up making a sound like a beached whale. My teacher made me practice after school, after everyone went home.

Just then the cake timer rang. I put on a mitt and opened the oven door. All the cupcakes in the pan were flat. They should have gotten nice and puffy as they cooked.

"Mom!" I yelled.

Mom rushed in a few seconds later. "Katie, what did I tell you about—oh," she said, looking at the deflated cupcakes.

"What happened?" I asked.

"This looks like a baking powder issue to me," she said. She put the pan of flat cupcakes on the counter and picked up the little can of baking powder. "Just as I thought. It's past its expiration date. You need fresh baking powder for your cupcakes to rise."

I felt terrible. "Sorry, guys."

"It's not your fault," Emma said.

"Yeah, and anyway, Eddie's not finished taking down that wallpaper yet," Mia said. "We can try again next time."

"Whenever that is," I mumbled.

Emma, Alexis, and Mia started picking up their things.

"We can talk about your grandma's cupcakes at lunch on Friday," Alexis said. "Everybody come with some ideas, okay?"

Emma saluted. "Yes, General Alexis!" she teased.

"Ooh, if Alexis is the general, can I be the Cupcake Captain?" I asked, and everyone laughed.

When my friends left, the kitchen was pretty quiet. Mom went into the den to do some paperwork, and all that was left was me and a pan of flat cupcakes.

As I cleaned up the mess, I thought of Alexis and Mia and Emma all going off and doing stuff—stuff that I couldn't do. They were all multitalented, and the only thing I could do was cupcakes. It made me feel a little bit lonely and a little bit like a loser.

In fact, it made me feel as flat as those cupcakes.

Still Hungry?

There's always room for another Cupcake!

Katie and the Cupcake Cure
978-1-4424-2275-9 $5.99
978-1-4424-2276-6 (eBook)

Mia in the Mix
978-1-4424-2277-3 $5.99
978-1-4424-2278-0 (eBook)

Emma on Thin Icing
978-1-4424-2279-7 $5.99
978-1-4424-2280-3 (eBook)

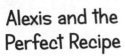

Alexis and the Perfect Recipe

978-1-4424-2901-7 $5.99
978-1-4424-2902-4 (eBook)

Katie, Batter Up!

978-1-4424-4611-3 $5.99
978-1-4424-4612-0 (eBook)

Mia's Baker's Dozen

978-1-4424-4613-7 $5.99
978-1-4424-4614-4 (eBook)

Emma All Stirred Up!

978-1-4424-5078-3 $5.99
978-1-4424-5079-0 (eBook)

Alexis Cool as a Cupcake

978-1-4424-5080-6 $5.99
978-1-4424-5081-3 (eBook)

Katie and the Cupcake War

978-1-4424-5373-9 $5.99
978-1-4424-5374-6 (eBook)

Mia's Boiling Point

978-1-4424-5396-8 $5.99
978-1-4424-5397-5 (eBook)

Emma, Smile and Say "Cupcake!"

978-1-4424-5398-2 $5.99
978-1-4424-5400-2 (eBook)